The Lightning Kid

When William Brookshire's son goes astray, the wealthy Dallas business owner hires veteran tracker, Rance Dehner, to ensure he is brought home safely. There is only one catch; William is sure that his son Thad is the notorious criminal, The Lightning Kid.

Now in a race against time to reach the boy before others get to him first, Rance is tossed into a whirlwind of death and deceit as he tries desperately to rescue Thad and uncover the true identity of the Lightning Kid.

By the same author

Reverend Colt

The Lightning Kid

James Clay

ROBERT HALE · LONDON

First published in Great Britain 2015

ISBN 978-0-7198-1576-8

Robert Hale Limited
Clerkenwell House
Clerkenwell Green
London EC1R 0HT

www.halebooks.com

Typeset by
Derek Doyle & Associates, Shaw Heath
Printed and bound in Great Britain by
CPI Antony Rowe, Chippenham and Eastbourne

CHAPTER ONE

Thad Brookshire made his way hastily down the boardwalk of Tin Cup, Texas. The laughter that blared from the Gold Coin Saloon sounded like mockery aimed at him. Anger raged inside the young man as the encounter from yesterday afternoon played in his mind.

Jed Coogan had been sitting at his large roll-top desk when he opened up the cash box and handed Thad a few bills. 'There's what I owe ya, boy. Good luck.'

'But sir, I haven't done anything wrong. I learned my job quickly and I've worked hard.'

The rotund, middle-aged man nodded his head. 'Yep, I know all that. But I still gotta let ya go. It's about that fight ya had with Ned Malloy.'

'Mr Coogan, I didn't want to fight Ned. He's been picking on me since the day I started work. I've ignored him. But yesterday he knocked me down for no reason. I had to get up and hit back.'

'I know all that, too.' Coogan replied. 'Ya didn't start it and ya finished it good. That's to your credit. But you're the one I gotta turn loose.'

'Why?'

Coogan gave the young man a sad smile. 'Nothin' wrong

with what ya do, boy, but you're different. Ya talk different and ya act different. Educated like. I'm sure that's what put a bug in Ned's ear. Now, Ned, he's one of the bunch. He fits in. Ya'll never fit in. So, light a shuck. I've a heap of work ta do 'fore nightfall.'

As he continued his walk down the boardwalk, Thad wondered if his fight with Ned Malloy had become fodder for bar-room gossip. He didn't know, but he did know he hadn't been able to find work at the two ranches he had stopped at earlier in the day.

The young man felt better when he saw a light beaming from Donahue's General Store. The place was still open. Good. He would buy some supplies and leave Tin Cup that night. He'd camp outside town and be on his way at sun-up: no sense spending money for a hotel room.

He'd leave in the morning. But leave for where?

As Brookshire approached the store, he heard a high-pitched pleading voice coming from inside. 'Please, I don't take in much money here—'

A shrill demand aborted the plea. 'Well, you jus' git that cashbox, Mister storeowner, and we'll see for ourselfs how much loot you got.'

Thad moved quickly but quietly to the store's open door. Four men with bandannas pulled over the bottom half of their faces held guns on Skeet Donahue, a short man with white hair that made him look older than his twenty-eight years. Thad reckoned Skeet was telling the truth about not having much cash. The storeowner was known for his generosity in extending credit.

The gunmen faced Donahue in a half-moon formation. Their backs were to the front door. Skeet stood a few feet in front of the store's counter. He made one last desperate attempt at talking the thieves out of their demands. 'You gotta understand, folks in Tin Cup depend on this store, they need us to give them time to pay up on—'

'I tole you to get the cash-box!' One of the gunmen slammed his pistol against the side of Skeet's head. Donahue spun sideways and dropped to his knees. He pushed himself up and back on to his feet, but began to stagger about as he did.

All four gunmen exploded with harsh laughter. The anger inside Thad Brookshire surged. The young man bolted into the store and delivered a hard punch to the face of one of the gunmen before any of the crooks could take further action. As his first victim went down, Thad swung a vicious kick into the knee of one of the other gunmen. His second victim screamed like a spanked child and bent over.

A hard force walloped Thad's head. He didn't know where it came from and, for the moment, it didn't seem to make any difference. A red screen seemed to block his vision and he fell to the floor. His sight returned in time for him to grab at a boot that was about to slam into his eye.

Brookshire twisted the ankle of his assailant, who plunged to the ground as Thad scrambled on to his feet and tried to take stock. The outlaws had holstered their guns, which had been employed to scare the storekeeper. They wanted to avoid gunplay if possible. Gunshots would bring the law.

Thad started to charge towards two of the thugs who were fighting with Skeet Donahue, but was tackled before he could reach them. He exchanged a flurry of punches with his new assailant and the momentum carried them out of the door and across the boardwalk where they toppled to the ground.

A shot sounded from inside the store, followed by a loud bellow of pain. Both Thad and his opponent experienced a sensation of fear and panic; the rules of engagement had just been brutally altered.

Three outlaws ran from the store, guns holstered. As they scrambled towards their horses that were tied to the hitch rail in front of the store, one of them shouted at Thad's assailant. 'Come on! We gotta get outta here!'

Thad Brookshire lay on the ground feeling a spark of relief. The thug who had been punching him was now running off. The spark was extinguished by a fast exchange of voices.

'What 'bout the kid?'

'Kill him. Maybe he can identify us.'

'But—'

'The store owner's already dead, kill him!'

An eerie sense of calm possessed Thad Brookshire. He saw the outlaw standing beside the hitch rail begin to go for his gun. Thad moved into a sitting position as he drew his .44 and squeezed the trigger. The outlaw twirled and his gun sailed into the sky, it span three times before landing several feet from the fallen outlaw, who was left squirming in the dust.

The other outlaws paused in a moment of confusion, uncertain about helping their fallen comrade.

The matter was settled by a loud, sharp voice. 'Freeze! Nobody move!'

The three remaining thugs drew their weapons and a nightmarish tangle of red spears flamed through the night.

Foster Lewis sat in the lobby of the Tin Cup Hotel, hoping someone would walk in that he could interview. Lewis had just wasted two hours in the Gold Coin Saloon talking with Wyatt Earp, or, as it turned out, a man who claimed to be Wyatt Earp. The reporter realized he had been tricked when someone shouted, 'Earl, how many free drinks have ya conned outta that fool writer?'

Foster left the saloon to the sound of raucous shouts. He had been the butt of a cruel joke. Nothing new. Lewis had spent much of his life being the butt of jokes.

The reporter pulled nervously at his beard. He was a medium-sized man in his early thirties. Foster had thinning brown hair, a spade beard and a pencil mustache. The facial hair looked awkward on his pale complexion, making him look like a boy dressing in his father's clothes.

His evening in the Gold Coin had been all too typical of this trip. He had little to show for his three weeks of touring western towns. Soon he would be facing an angry editor.

A tall thin man with rotting teeth and a nose that had been broken long ago slowly opened the front door of the hotel and then slipped inside, carrying a jug. Lewis immediately spotted the gent as a moonshiner selling his wares.

Unlike Foster, the moonshiner was enjoying a touch of good luck. The desk clerk had stepped out for a few minutes. Foster was the only other person in the lobby.

The newcomer approached Lewis quickly. 'Evenin', the name's Boone Estey.' Boone's black hair fell over his shoulders and his beard was unkempt. There wasn't a touch of grey in all that thick hair. Boone was younger than he first appeared, he was still in his teens, Lewis reckoned.

'Good evening, I'm Foster Lewis.' Foster leaned back in his chair, trying to escape the odor that oozed from the moonshiner.

Boone spoke hurriedly, the desk clerk would soon be back and he'd be ordered out. 'Got somethin' here you'll like.' He patted the jug.

'How much?'

'Only—'

A shot sounded from up the street. Lewis bolted from his

chair and ran out of the hotel's front door. Standing on the boardwalk, he could see three men hurrying to mount horses which were tied up at a hitch rail.

Another shot sent a loud bellow through the night followed by the neighing of terrified horses. Lewis took a few steps forward, trying to ascertain where the second shot had come from.

'Look out!' The reporter was pushed aside as a figure ran by him, drawing his gun. Foster Lewis trotted at a safe distance behind the gunman as he charged between the murky puddles of light that fell on the boardwalk from several windows.

Boone Estey leaned against the hotel's false front and waited. Sooner or later, that Foster fella would return to the hotel.

'Maybe I'll get me a sale after all,' he spoke aloud to an indifferent, dark sky.

CHAPTER TWO

Rance Dehner stood on the porch of one of Dallas' finest homes and watched his boss reach up to employ the knocker on the ornate front door in front of them. The detective anticipated a greeting from an elderly butler and so was surprised when a beautiful young girl of about sixteen opened the door.

'Good morning, Mr Lowrie. Good to see you again.' The young woman smiled at Rance's employer. The smile was subdued, but still communicated a ton of charm.

'The pleasure is mine, Sally,' came the courteous, old school reply. 'And this is my associate, Mr Rance Dehner.'

Dehner exchanged a 'How do you do,' with the girl, who quickly got to the point. 'Father is expecting you. I'll take you to him.'

The two detectives followed Sally's brisk footsteps as she guided them past a curved stairway and down a wide hall. They walked past two women wearing identical dresses, who were engaged in dusting a line of paintings that decorated both walls. The women were being slow and methodical in what was obviously a delicate undertaking. Sally stopped in front of the last door in the hallway, where a muscular man of about five and a half feet was stepping out.

'Is Father ready to receive visitors, Tom?'

'Yes, Miss Sally.'

'Thank you, oh—' Sally Brookshire apologized for her lapse in manners and introduced the two detectives to Tom, whom she described as her father's 'head assistant'.

Dehner figured Tom had a variety of responsibilities. From what the detective's boss had told him, the 'assistants' were the only healthy, strong men in a house that contained a fortune in artwork alone.

Sally escorted them into a room where three of the walls were covered by bookshelves, several of them in a state of disorder. Obviously, the tomes were frequently removed and read. The room was dominated by a desk and even more so by the man who sat behind it.

'Good morning, Bert. Good to see you again.'

Bertram Lowrie pressed his lips together. He hated being called 'Bert'. But the pained expression on the tall, thin man's face was short-lived. 'Likewise, William.'

Dehner noted the heavy formality in his boss's voice.

Bertram Lowrie and William Brookshire were on a first name basis, but the relationship was still one of employee and employer.

Mr Brookshire gave his daughter a quick glance. 'Thank you, Sally. That will be all for now.'

Sally smiled and exited. The girl seemed to fill the job of secretary. Dehner wondered if the position ever contradicted her role as daughter.

After she departed, Lowrie immediately spoke up. Three years in Texas had not dented his British accent. 'As per your request, William, I have brought along my associate, Mr Rance Dehner.'

Brookshire extended his right hand. 'Good to meet you, Rance. I apologize for not getting up.'

Rance shook hands with a man who presented a striking contrast: William Brookshire's face was still that of a young man. There were wrinkles at the corners of his eyes, but nowhere else. His sandy hair was thick, with only slight streaks of gray decorating the areas around his ears. The rest of his body, though, looked frail and almost too thin for the wheelchair that held it. A blanket was draped across his lap.

'Do you gentlemen believe in an afterlife?' Brookshire asked.

Bertram Lowrie's head snapped back as if he had been slapped. 'I was raised in the Church of England,' he declared.

Neither of the other two men in the room knew how to interpret that last remark. Dehner hastily chimed in, 'I was raised a Baptist. I'm not a very good one, but yes, I believe in an afterlife.'

'I know the question is a bit odd,' Brookshire shot Lowrie an apologetic look. 'But my doctor has informed me that . . . well . . . I'm not a religious man, but I suppose I'd better start doing some thinking about my soul.'

William Brookshire paused and looked about restlessly as if trying to think about his soul, but not knowing where to begin. He again glanced at Lowrie, 'Have you told Rance about my . . . situation?'

'No. I have followed your instructions in this matter.'

Brookshire nodded his head approvingly and turned to Rance. 'I entered the war between the states when I was eighteen. Thought war would be a lot of fun. Found out different. I came back in '63 with my right leg gone and my left one worthless.'

'I'm sorry,' Rance spoke in soft voice.

William Brookshire smiled and his voice boomed. 'Life has been good to me. I gave up on my dream of being a cowboy and became a businessman instead.' He threw up his hands, gesturing at all that was around him. 'As you can see, it worked out pretty well.'

The businessman dropped his hands and his voice quieted. 'Well, not everything went so well.'

'What do you mean, sir?' Dehner realized they were getting close to the purpose behind this meeting.

'I have two kids. You've met Sally, she's the youngest. My son, Thaddeaus, is eighteen. Their mother died when Thad was seven. I've tried to be a good father to them. Sally and I get along fine, but I guess it is hard for a boy to have a father in a wheelchair who spends his days behind a desk.'

Brookshire looked away from the two detectives, but only for a moment. He was a man who looked others in the eye, to do less was, for him, improper. 'I talked a lot to Thad about my war experiences. I talked too much, I guess. Thad and I didn't get along very well the last couple of years. He ran off nine months ago.'

'Have you heard anything from him or about him since?'

Dehner asked.

William Brookshire pulled out the middle drawer of his desk and handed Rance a magazine. *Real Gunfighters* was the kind of publication still known as a penny dreadful, even though the price was now two cents. The cover featured a crude drawing of a gunfight in a dusty street of a western town, where one man was gunning down four. The caption proclaimed, *The Coming of The Lightning Kid!*

'When he was in school, my son loved to race,' Brookshire explained. 'His pals gave him the nickname, "Lightning".'

'You think your son is The Lightning Kid?!'

The businessman nodded his head. 'That magazine arrived in the mail last week. There was no return address.'

Dehner read the article inside. The writer, Foster Lewis, claimed that in the town of Tin Cup, Texas four outlaws had tried looting supplies from a local General Store. One of the thugs began to pistol whip the owner. A stranger walked into the store and promptly decked the offender with a hard right. A loud argument ensued, and the four outlaws challenged the stranger to meet them in the street. He did, and in the gunfight that followed, he killed all four outlaws.

When the sheriff arrived, he asked for the stranger's name and, according to Foster, the gunman replied, 'Just call me the Lightning Kid!'

Like everything else in *Real Gunfighters* the writing was crude and the article short. Dehner turned to the title page and discovered the magazine was published in Dallas. 'We can go to the office of *Real Gunfighters*, and—'

Brookshire smiled good naturedly. 'I believe your boss has already taken care of that, right Bert?'

'Yes, I visited the offices of *Thrilling Adventures Publications* yesterday.'

Dehner couldn't tell if the tone of disapproval in his boss' voice came from disgust with the magazine or displeasure at being called 'Bert.' Probably a bit of both.

'What did you find out?' Rance asked.

'I talked with Mr Foster Lewis, who, by the way, does resemble that drawing of him which accompanies the article.'

Dehner nudged his employer on, 'What did Lewis tell you?'

'The description he gave of the Lightning Kid matches that of Thad Brookshire: tall, sandy hair, well over six feet, about 185 pounds—'

William Brookshire anxiously cut in, 'Did you ask him about the boy's age?'

'Yes, and what the so-called writer told me seemed quite acceptable. At first, Mr Lewis assumed the boy was in his early twenties, but after talking to him he became less certain. Yes, The Lightning Kid might be eighteen.'

'Was the story about the gunfight true?' Rance chimed in.

'Mr Lewis claimed it was.'

'Did you look into it further?' Dehner wasn't really asking a question.

'I did indeed query Mr Lewis' background. His reputation is somewhat blemished, but not altogether without merit. Foster Lewis rarely makes anything up from whole cloth, but he does embellish.' Lowrie looked directly at his client. 'Your son was, in all likelihood, involved in an altercation that began in a General Store and ended in the streets of Tin Cup. Whether he killed four men or any men at all remains a matter to be clarified.'

'I understand that you have had previous business in Tin Cup, Mr Dehner, and you know the sheriff there,' the businessman continued.

'Yes. His name is Harry Clausen and he's a fine man.'

'When can you leave?'

Rance shrugged his shoulders and began to speak, 'Any—'

'Immediately!' Lowrie cut in. 'I have already assigned other operatives to Mr Dehner's current case load.'

Rance suppressed a chuckle. His boss had just prevented him from revealing that he didn't have a case load. However, his new assignment did have him confused. 'What exactly do you want me to do in Tin Cup?'

'Find my son!' Desperation laced Brookshire's voice. He paused for a moment, then continued in a calm manner that was obviously hard for him. 'Then bring Thad home. He doesn't have to stay here. I just want to talk to my son before . . . you see the doctors say I have about a year. . . .'

Brookshire's face contorted and he looked away from his guests. Bertram Lowrie immediately spoke up. 'Mr Dehner will be leaving for Tin Cup first thing tomorrow. We are very optimistic that Thaddeus will be back home soon, William.'

Dehner nodded his head in silent agreement. This job seemed pretty easy. Thad Brookshire ran away from home at the age of eighteen, the same age his father had been when he enlisted in the war between the states. Thad now called himself the Lightning Kid, a name that would be immediately recognized by his family. Dehner felt sure Thad had sent his father that copy of *Real Gunfighters.*

The situation was common enough, a young man rebelling against his father and, at the same time, trying desperately to impress him. Rance figured he had a simple job that would, no doubt, pay good money.

A sense of unease suddenly gripped the detective. He remembered previous times when he had thought he was being given an easy assignment.

It never seemed to work out that way.

CHAPTER THREE

Thad Brookshire took off his apron and tossed it on to the counter of Donahue's General Store. 'This is the second time I've been fired since coming to Tin Cup.'

Thad had intended the remark as a joke, but Skeet Donahue looked genuinely hurt. 'You're not bein' fired. It's jus' that. . . .'

Skeet's wife, Emma, picked up the thread. 'My husband is back on his feet now, Thad, and we can't afford to keep you on. I sure wish we could.' She pointed at a wooden rack that held books, magazines and newspapers. 'Since that magazine came out our store has been known as the place where you can meet the Lightning Kid.'

'I'll be very happy when folks forget about the Lightning Kid.' Thad didn't mean what he said, but thought it sounded good.

'Emma and me is real sorry we can't. . . .'

This time, Thad decided on a more serious approach. He spoke as he put on his gun belt. 'You both told me the job was temporary when I was hired. I'm just happy to see you healthy again, Skeet. One of those gunmen said you were dead. And when I saw you lying on the floor I thought for sure you were gone.'

Thad cringed inwardly. He had kicked the wrong can again. Emma's eyes became moist and she gripped her husband's arm. The next few moments were an awkward exchange of pleasantries as Emma insisted that Thad have dinner with them once a week. After agreeing to do so, Thad hurried out of the store.

As he made his way to the Gold Coin Saloon the young man mused on how this situation was so different from the last time he got fired, a little more than two months back. He had been happy to go to work for the Donahues even though the pay wasn't much. They were good people. Part of his pay had included a comfortable cot to sleep on at night, and he ate all his meals with Skeet and Emma.

Then, three weeks back, that magazine came out and everything changed. The hotel offered him a free room, which he turned down, and Hugh Corry told him, 'Anytime ya get the notion, come by Corry's Café and get yourself a free meal.'

Thad paused in front of the Gold Coin as two men came out, patted him on the shoulder and told him how great it was to have the Lightning Kid in Tin Cup. Thad entered the saloon and walked directly to the bar where the barkeep began to pour a beer for him: a beer that would be on the house.

'Thanks Otto,' Thad had really wanted a sarsaparilla and planned to ask for one. But first he had to deal with the mug in front of him. A quick sip revealed that the stuff tasted awful, and contrary to what the sign outside claimed, it wasn't even cold.

He knew a lot of eyes were on him and tried not to make a face as he returned the mug to the bar. How long could this last? For that matter, how long did he want it to last? He missed Dallas and his family and wondered if they had realized that the Lightning Kid was Thad Brookshire when they read the issue of *Real Gunfighters* he had sent them.

He glanced briefly at Pop Cummings, half of whose torso was spread out on one of the saloon's round tables. Pop got drunk and passed out every night of the week. Old man Cummings had fought in the war between the states, or told people he had. Thad thought Pop's war stories were for the most part true and wondered at the ways fighting a war could effect a man. His father had certainly handled it differently to Pop.

'I hear tell you're the Lightning Kid!'

Thad turned around to face a wiry, nervous man who had just stepped through the Gold Coin's batwing doors. He was wearing new clothes complete with boots that looked a bit odd; Thad guessed the boots were padded to give the wearer an inch or two of height.

More important than the boots was the shiny Colt .45 strapped to the newcomer's waist. Thad pegged the man's age at a touch past twenty.

'Yeah, some folks call me the Lightning Kid.' Thad's voice was a monotone. 'What's your handle?'

'I'm called Bronco, 'cause of how I can tame a wild horse.'

'Good to meet you, Bronco.'

'I ain't so happy to meet you.'

Thad knew where this was leading, but didn't know how to stop it. 'Why's that?'

'I come by my name honest like. I think you're jus' a lot of thunder, yeah, you're jus' a lotta noise. No lightning 'bout your way with a gun.'

Thad wondered at the atmosphere inside the saloon. The bartender, saloon girls and customers were almost salivating with anticipation. Thad realized this was what it was really all about: the free drinks, restaurant meals and the rest. Folks wanted a show. No one in the saloon gave the slightest thought to talking Bronco out of his recklessness. They wanted a gunfight where one man lay dead in a pool of blood.

This was different from stopping thieves who were robbing a store and beating up the owner. This was needless killing.

Thad Brookshire took a final look at the crowd, who were now lined against the walls watching with eager eyes. Only Pop Cummings remained where he was. 'Go back to your horses, Bronco,' Thad's voice almost broke.

Bronco laughed mockingly. 'Why, I believe the Lightning Kid is about to cry! Guess you got something to cry about!'

Bronco did everything wrong. He inhaled deeply and his eyebrows sprung up before he reached for his gun. Thad got off the first shot before his opponent had cleared leather. The Lightning Kid had aimed for the chest, but the bullet ripped into Bronco's neck. Bronco made a grotesque, gurgling sound as he dropped to the floor. The crowd watched in silence as the dying man thrust about and then went limp.

Thad walked cautiously towards his fallen adversary. He crouched over and picked up the .45 which lay beside the dead youth. As Thad stood back up he could hear footsteps running toward the saloon. Sheriff Harry Clausen burst inside and stopped at the dead body.

Everything about Clausen seemed like a contradiction to Thad. The sheriff was a middle-aged man whose hair and moustache were the colour of salt and pepper. He walked with a slight limp. And, yet, the lawman always seemed strong, nimble and fast.

Harry Clausen quickly examined the corpse, then gave Thad a harsh glare. 'Is this your handiwork?'

'Yes, sir,' Thad Brookshire's voice was a slight whisper. He handed the sheriff the Colt.

The harshness in Clausen's eyes vanished. He stared at Thad for a moment, then looked at the bartender while nodding his head at the dead body. 'Can you handle this, Otto?'

'Sure Sheriff, no problem.' Otto called out the names of two men, promising them free drinks if they got the body to the town's barber, who was also the undertaker.

One of the patrons in the saloon shouted, 'Don't blame the Lightning Kid, Sheriff! The other guy went for his gun first, but the kid was too fast for him!'

Pop Cummings sat up in his chair and looked about stupidly. The rest of the crowd began to return to the bar and tables to continue the night's revelry. Men slapped Thad on the back and proclaimed, 'Ain't never seen no one faster,' and similar compliments. Thad felt ill.

'Come on, boy.' Thad followed the sheriff out of the saloon and down the boardwalk. He felt increasingly nauseous. As Clausen opened the door to his office, Thad stepped off the boardwalk and vomited. The lawman pretended not to notice. He stepped inside the office and placed the .45 on his desk.

Harry Clausen spoke in a low voice as the young man entered the office. 'It's an awful feelin', ain't it?'

Thad nodded his head. 'Why did Bronco do it?'

'Bronco?'

'The man I . . . the man I killed. He told me his name was Bronco.'

A wistful expression covered the sheriff's face. 'I always knew him as Larry Horton. He was a ranch hand for Art Sherman.'

'He told me folks called him Bronco because of how he could tame wild horses.'

Clausen shrugged his shoulders. 'He might have broken a bronc or two, guess it really doesn't make much difference now.'

'But why. . . .'

'Larry, or Bronco, was there that day you shot one of the thugs who was tryin' to rob the general store. Remember seein' him standin' around when I got there.'

'So?'

The sheriff continued, 'Larry probably read that magazine. Thought if you could be a famous gunfighter, he could be more famous for killin' you.'

'I should have never mouthed off to that writer! What got into me?'

'You surely did help Skeet Donahue when those saddle tramps tried to loot his store.' The sheriff made a fist, 'From what Skeet says, you jumped right in.'

'You know I still don't remember exactly what happened. One of them knocked me down and we ended up in the street in front of the store. He got up and pulled a gun, so I pulled mine and fired. He screamed something awful and went down. Then. . . .'

'Then I came along,' Harry Clausen said. 'I shot one of the other thugs. You fired again but missed. Then they got scared plenty and surrendered. The two who took bullets recovered. All four of them fellas are now in the state prison.'

'Where did that fool writer come from, anyway?'

'He was in the hotel lobby. He heard all the ruckus and came runnin'.'

Thad Brookshire gave an angry sigh. He was angry with himself. 'That writer kept putting words in my mouth and I went along. But that part about the Lightning Kid, I made that up myself.'

To Brookshire's relief the sheriff did not ask him why he had chosen the name 'Lightning Kid'. What the sheriff did ask surprised him: 'How would you like to be my deputy?'

'What?'

'I've been needin' a deputy for some time now. I've seen you handle a gun. You're good for someone who ain't had much in the way of trainin'. I could help you out.'

'I'm not sure. . . .'

'There's somethin' else to think about.'

'What's that?'

'Like it or not, you're gettin' a reputation as a gunfighter. That magazine is tellin' everyone you outgunned four men. Now, who knows what kind of tales will get around about you out drawin' Bronco.'

Thad looked downward, 'Oh brother. . . .'

'Becomin' a deputy might nip some of that in the bud. A fool kid or two bit thug will think twice before challengin' a man wearing a piece of tin. Most of the time, anyhow.'

The young man was silent for a moment. He ended the silence with a nod of his head, 'OK, I'll try it, for a while at least. . . .'

Thad looked around the office and gave his surroundings a smile of wonderment. 'I never would have guessed. . . .'

'What do you mean?'

'I mean, I'm going to be trained to be a deputy by a real western sheriff.'

A slight tinge of red covered Clausen's face. He pulled out a side drawer of his desk, grabbed a badge and spoke officiously as he pinned it on Thad's shirt. 'I'll swear you in now and you can come with me on a round. Tomorrow mornin' I'll take you out of town and show you how to use a gun proper like. Get as much sleep as you can tonight.'

'Why?'

'A lawman doesn't sleep much.'

CHAPTER FOUR

'So, the Lightning Kid is packin' a star!' Otto the bartender spoke loudly, allowing everyone in the Gold Coin to hear him. Otto had a large forehead which jutted out over his eyes, giving them a permanently dark appearance. 'I guess now we should call you Deputy Lightning.'

Good natured laughter bounced across the saloon. Thad Brookshire spoke in a voice equal to that of Otto. 'Just call me deputy, or Deputy Brookshire or Thad, I've had enough of the Lightning Kid!' This time, Thad meant what he said.

'Well, Thad, it's about time we got on with our round!' Harry Clausen's eyes skirted the saloon. 'Go easy on my new deputy, boys, at least for a spell. I don't want him to quit on me!' More laughter followed as Harry and Thad left the saloon.

Beau Haney didn't laugh. He didn't even look up from the table in an isolated corner of the Gold Coin where he sat alone staring into a drink. What had been the name of the saloon owner who had been a friend of his when he was the sheriff of Tin Cup? As he took another sip of whiskey, he reckoned it didn't make much difference. The guy was dead and nobody was his friend now.

The former lawman finished his drink, got up from the table and weaved his way out of the saloon. No one took notice.

Haney whispered curses at the people he passed on the boardwalk as he shuffled towards his house: a house that had been built back in the day when he ruled Tin Cup. He slowed his steps as he moved closer to the edge of town and away from the kerosene lights.

A large mesquite tree stood a few yards to the side of Beau Haney's house. Haney enjoyed passing under that tree. The mesquite was one of the few items from his past that didn't deride his present.

He heard the sound of rapid footsteps and looked about in a confused daze before a fist slammed into his face and sent him plunging to the ground, just barely missing the trunk of the mesquite. A loud, high pitched laugh pierced Haney's ears and the long barrel of a six shooter pressed against his forehead as a dark figure crouched over him.

'Not the tough guy you used to be, are you, Beau?'

'Who . . . who are you?'

'A man with a good memory. A man who remembers when you were strong instead of a ton of blubber. A man you killed.'

Haney's lawman instincts had been diluted by alcohol, but not totally washed away. He tried to look beyond the gun barrel to the man holding the weapon. The tree's thick foliage blocked most of the light the stars and moon offered. All he could see of his assailant was a bandanna that covered half of his face, a flat crowned hat pulled low and a duster that curtained most of his clothes.

Haney tried to inject a sense of bravado into his voice as he spoke. 'A man I killed! Ya must be more drunk than I am!'

The tormentor delivered a hard slap to Haney's face and sent more pain searing through his head. 'You're the rummy, Beau, not me. I never got the chance to become a worthless souse. I was twenty when you and a few other good citizens murdered me, and it was twenty years ago. Remember?'

Haney remembered. 'Jimmy . . . Jimmy Ellis.'

'That's right, Beau.'

'Impossible . . . can't. . . .'

'Don't you worry about that part, Beau. I got a little job for you.'

'Maybe I don't wanna do no job for a dead man.'

Ellis pulled back the hammer on his pistol.

'No, please Jimmy, I'll do it!'

A harsh laugh scorched Haney's soul like a branding iron. 'Big Beau Haney, Tin Cup's tough sheriff. You're nothing but an old fat man now, Beau!'

'Jimmy . . . please . . . jus' tell me what ya want.'

'You're going to be my messenger.'

'Whatta ya mean?'

'You tell all the fine citizens of Tin Cup who took part in my murder that Jimmy Ellis has come back from hell. Tell them they're going to be joining me there very soon.'

'You're gonna kill us!?'

'Just deliver the message, old man.' The dark figure stood up, began to walk away, then stopped and turned around. 'Oh, one more thing, Beau. Here's a little memento, just for old time's sake.' He tossed a small object at the former lawman.

Jimmy Ellis vanished into the darkness. Haney crawled over to where the object had landed and picked it up. With one hand a fist, he continued to crawl until he was out from under the blackness provided by the thick branches of the tree.

With the light the sky now offered him, Haney opened his fist and stared at the object that lay there. What he saw caused him to tremble. He lay on the ground and whimpered like a kicked dog. Haney didn't know when he fell asleep, but a sun the color of fire cut through his closed eyes and forced him awake.

'Hell is coming for me,' he shouted.

CHAPTER FIVE

As Rance Dehner rode into the town of Tin Cup he first observed the things that hadn't changed. Tin Cup sat on flat land but it was surrounded by hills. Bordering the town on the east were mountains that shot up defiantly like the fists of angry devils. The detective then took in the things that had changed. Most noticeable was a series of freshly printed flyers, posted just about everywhere, announcing a meeting of the Temperance Union which was to take place the next Monday.

As Dehner continued his ride toward Abbot's Livery, he spotted a familiar face: Otto Snider, the bartender at the Gold Coin Saloon. The last time Rance had visited the Gold Coin he had, in a reversal of the way these matters usually go, listened to the bartender unleash a sad story of how he had been betrayed by a woman he loved.

Otto's problems with the gentler sex seemed to be continuing. The bartender was arguing with two ladies who were nailing a flyer to a post outside of Barlow's Hardware Store.

'What you want ain't natural!' Otto shouted. 'A man needs a drink, now and again. . . .'

'We don't need any lectures from you, Mr Snider!' one of the ladies shot back. 'We don't put much stock in the opinions of a man who earns a dirty dollar selling drinks that destroy souls!'

Dehner gently spurred his bay into a trot. The good citizens of Tin Cup could argue their differences without any assistance from him.

Rance dismounted in front of the livery and walked his horse in. He engaged in some friendly jawing with the proprietors Stanley Abbot and his son, then left his horse in the care of the Hostlers. Dehner was only a few yards away from the livery and less than a minute into his search for Thad Brookshire when a voice sounded behind him.

'Ah, hey, mister, ain't you Dehner, . . . ah . . . Rance Dehner?'

A heavy-set man emerged from the livery, trying to move fast. His voice sounded winded as he caught up with Rance. 'You're a detective with the Lowrie Agency, ain't ya?'

Rance felt embarrassed. The man now standing beside him looked familiar, but Dehner couldn't place his name or even remember when he had last seen him. 'Well, yes, I'm with the Lowrie—'

'My name's Beau Haney. We met the last time ya were here. Remember? Harry Clausen introduced ya to me. I usta be sheriff.'

'Yes, of course. Good to see you again, Beau.' Not really. Beau Haney's face was pale and his hands were shaking. He looked like a desperate man.

Haney gestured nervously toward the Livery. 'I do some chores for Stanley. Make a little extra money.'

Rance nodded his head.

The smile on Beau's face became increasingly forced. 'Wonder if ya could do me a little favor, Rance. . . .'

'What do you have in mind?'

'Something happened to me last night. Something pretty crazy. The sheriff needs to hear 'bout it.'

'Where do I fit in?'

'Well, ya know Harry Clausen, he's a good lawdog.'

Dehner again nodded his head.

'But Clausen don't have much imagination.' Haney paused and his smile vanished. 'I'm a man who likes his drink, the sheriff might not see past that. I thought maybe . . . being a detective from Dallas and all . . . maybe ya could make some sense outta what happened to me.'

Rance had originally thought that Haney's trembling came from his need for a drink. The detective changed that assessment. Beau Haney was terrified.

'Tell you what, Beau. I was heading for the sheriff's office anyway. No reason we can't go there together. If it's all right with Harry, I'm OK with listening in on anything you have to say to the sheriff.'

The terror didn't leave Haney, but it was diminished by a slight touch of hope. 'Sure, Rance, that'll be great. Thanks.'

The two men walked in silence to the sheriff's office. On the way, Dehner exchanged waves with a few people he recognized from his last visit to Tin Cup. Outside the door of the office he could hear laughter and the voice of a young man. 'So, then Clem said, "If you're Mr Law in these here parts, order God to strike me dead."

There was more laughter, then a voice Dehner recognized as Harry Clausen said, 'What'd you do next?'

'I told him, "Clem, God doesn't need to waste any thunderbolts on you. I can knock you over and drag you to jail with one hand. Now, get on your mule and go home".'

Laughter exploded once again, but subsided as Dehner and Haney entered the office. At first, Harry Clausen's face reflected irritation, as if the two men had barged into his home and interrupted a private conversation, but the lawman quickly recovered. He stood up from where he had been sitting behind his desk and held out his hand. 'Well, Rance Dehner, good to see you, and it's always nice havin' the former sheriff drop by.'

There were introductions all around. Dehner became excited when he realized he had found Thad Brookshire less than an hour after arriving in town. But he kept his excitement in check. His real mission was to get Thad to return home. The detective sensed that this was not the time to even discuss the matter with the young man.

Harry Clausen seemed to assume Rance was just stopping by Tin Cup to renew some past friendships after finishing a case somewhere else. Rance decided not to correct that notion.

'I gotta tell ya, something, Harry.'

Clausen looked at Beau Haney carefully. The sheriff's demeanor became grim but he tried to keep his voice casual. 'Sure, Beau.' He pointed at a battered wooden chair in front of the desk. 'Sit down and tell us what's on your mind.'

Listening to Haney's story of his encounter with the ghost of Jimmy Ellis, Dehner was as fascinated by the reaction of the sheriff to the story as he was by the tale itself. Contrary to Beau's earlier fears, the lawman didn't seem to believe the ghost story was the ravings of a drunk.

Thad Brookshire's reaction was one of total confusion. Dehner could identify with that.

Silence followed Beau Haney's account. Dehner broke it with a question. 'This object you say Jimmy Ellis tossed at you, what was it?'

Haney unbuttoned the pocket of his shirt, pulled out a coin and handed it to Rance. The detective looked at the round piece of silver which boasted an impression of a seated Lady Liberty. 'Why would a ghost give you a half dollar?'

The question was addressed to Beau Haney, who remained silent. Clausen sighed deeply and spoke. 'Twenty years ago, Jimmy Ellis started shootin' up the town one night.'

'Why?' That was the first word Thad had spoken since Beau began his strange account.

'Jimmy didn't need a reason to destroy people or things. He just did it.'

'Was Mr Haney the sheriff back then?' Thad asked.

The sheriff paused. Hearing Beau Haney referred to as 'Mr Haney' seemed to surprise him. 'Yes, Beau was the sheriff and I was his deputy. Between us, we managed to bring Jimmy down without shootin' him. Beau served as a decoy while I tackled him from behind.'

The anguished tone of Clausen's voice bothered Rance. He tried to sound comforting. 'Sounds like you and Beau handled the situation well, Harry.'

'Jimmy Ellis didn't think so,' Clausen replied. 'He began shoutin' curses at us.'

Haney raised one of his shaking hands. 'That's when I done it. I said, "For a saddle bum who ain't worth a sawbuck, ya sure do a lot of jawing".'

That remark sounded harmless to Dehner and the young deputy, but Harry Clausen shook his head before speaking. 'By then, a crowd had gathered. They started laughing. They laughed loud. Real loud. Jimmy went completely loco. He tried to break away from us. A few strong men from the crowd helped Beau and me restrain him and get him into a jail cell.'

Thad spoke softly. Like Rance, he sensed that there was a treacherous undertow to this story. 'What happened next?'

'Jimmy spent a few weeks in jail for disturbin' the peace,' the sheriff answered. 'The day he was turned loose, he shot a man down for callin' him "sawbuck". A week or so later Jimmy was dead.'

'Did—'

The door to the sheriff's office opened and Thad Brookshire lost interest in whatever question he was about to ask. Dehner could hardly blame him. The young woman who stepped inside was quite a distraction. She had long hair the color of straw, blue eyes and skin tanned to resemble honey. Her face was perfectly proportioned and looked as if it smiled most of the time.

The young woman wasn't smiling now. She paused for a moment, her eyes falling on Thad. She seemed to be taking as much interest in him as he did in her. But those blue eyes quickly shifted to Harry Clausen.

'I'm sorry if I interrupted something—'

The sheriff had caught the woman's tenseness. 'That's OK Amanda, what's up?'

'Jed Coogan's dead. He's been killed. Our ramrod, Leo Jensen, found him a few hours ago. He and Father brought the body into town. They are taking it to the undertaker now.'

Beau Haney screamed as he jumped up from his chair. 'He's doing what he said he would. Jimmy Ellis is—'

'Be quiet, Beau!' Clausen shouted, then lowered his voice. 'Amanda, what was one of your hands doing on Jed Coogan's spread?'

Amanda closed her eyes for a moment as if trying to calm herself. 'Leo found the body on our ranch. Near that old line shack on the south-west corner of our land. Mr Coogan had been shot and his body dumped under a cottonwood tree.'

Both the former and current sheriff looked at each other and then looked away as if sharing a shameful secret. When

Haney spoke his voice was a low whine. 'That cottonwood tree. It's where we murdered Jimmy Ellis, twenty years ago.'

CHAPTER SIX

When Harry Clausen returned to his office, his face was a stoic mask. Three men followed behind him: Rance Dehner, Leo Jensen, and Abner Shaw; the latter was the owner of the Rocking S Ranch and Amanda's father.

The sheriff stepped behind his desk and tossed a coin on it. 'A half dollar, found lyin' on top of Jed's corpse.' He glanced at Dehner, 'I guess you detectives would call that a clue.'

Rance shrugged his shoulders. 'I don't know what to call it.'

Abner Shaw leaned sideways on his cane. 'Harry, you don't believe all that fool talk Beau was babblin' about a ghost, do you?'

Before the lawman could reply, Leo Jensen blurted out, 'Don't laugh at ghosts, Mr Shaw. There's plenty of stuff going on in the world that we know nothing about.'

Dehner noted that Abner Shaw and his ramrod were a curious contrast. Shaw was a large, wide shouldered man with huge muscles. But those muscles seemed to be in a process of atrophy. Abner was very dependent on a large, heavy cane and his eyes would occasionally look confused and empty.

Leo Jensen was slim, with ropey muscles. He was a restless

man who seemed to find standing still difficult. Yet, he was very protective of his boss, always staying close by, apparently fearful that the old man could fall.

'I'll hold off when it comes to ghosts,' Clausen tried to sound cheerful as he looked at Abner and Leo. 'But I'll say this. I'm obliged to you two gents and Amanda for bringin' Jed's body into town. You've done all you can. Time to get back home. You've got a ranch to run.'

'He's right, Mr Shaw,' Leo said. 'We'd best be on our way. Amanda's already left.'

Abner Shaw rubbed his forehead intently as if massaging a headache. 'Jed's death, Beau's wild story, it all brings back such memories . . . terrible memories.'

'Yes sir,' Leo replied softly. 'Let's get home and get some good food into us.' The ramrod walked beside his boss as they slowly made their way out of the office.

Clausen picked up the half dollar from his desk, flipped it upwards and caught it. 'Rance, I got no right to ask this of you. But this Jimmy Ellis thing could drive the whole town loco. You've met my one deputy. He's a great kid but, well, he's a kid. Could you hang around and help me? I could make you a deputy . . . can't pay you—'

'I'll be a volunteer deputy, but I need something else besides money.'

'What?'

'Information. There's a story behind this Jimmy Ellis matter. I need to know what it is.'

The sheriff gestured to the chair in front of his desk, as he sat down behind it. 'Yes . . . of course. This is goin' to take a while.'

Thad Brookshire finished his meal at Corry's Café and exchanged a few pleasant words with Hugh Corry as he paid for his dinner. Hugh referred to him as 'deputy' and didn't even try to let him have the meal on the house. That's the way Thad wanted it. He was a lawman and no longer the Lightning Kid.

As he left the restaurant and approached his horse that stood tethered across the street, Thad felt less than content. He had not really been honest with the sheriff when he asked if he could 'call it a day' after viewing the corpse of Jed Coogan. Harry Clausen had looked surprised but said, 'Sure.' The sheriff probably thought his deputy was upset after looking at a murder victim whom he had recently worked for.

After patting his chestnut, Thad pulled a piece of paper from his shirt pocket and once again examined the hand drawn map. He then pulled out his pocket watch: time to head out. The deputy mounted his horse and rode out of town, hoping few people would see him.

The sky was a vast collage of red, blue and purple as Thad guided his horse up a large, horseshoe shaped hill and paused at the crest. He removed a telescope from one of his saddle bags and examined the land below. 'I'm at the right place,' the deputy whispered to himself.

The way down was rocky and steep. Thad rode carefully. As he reached the bottom of the hill, he dismounted and tied up his chestnut at the hitch rail in front of an old line shack. One other horse was already tethered there. The clapboard structure itself looked dilapidated and depressing, but that changed quickly when Amanda Shaw opened the front door.

'Thank you for coming. I'm sorry I was so mysterious when we talked back in Tin Cup, but there wasn't much time. You had to go and look at poor Mr Coogan's corpse and. . . .'

'I understand, Miss Shaw. And the map you gave me worked just fine.' Thad tried to quell his nervousness as he walked towards the open door of the cabin where the young woman remained standing. He had never before seen a woman as beautiful as Amanda Shaw.

The young man quickly got ahold of himself and tried to sound official. 'Miss Shaw, you told me you had important information on Jed Coogan's murder. Why didn't you just give that information to the sheriff?'

Amanda Shaw looked down, taking a sudden interest in her hands. 'I wasn't exactly truthful with you.' When her face turned upward, it held a pleading look. 'But, you've got to understand, my father could be the next victim and nobody around here wants to talk about what's really going on.'

Thad shrugged his shoulders. 'What is really going on?'

'I don't know!' Amanda threw up her arms and began to wander away from the cabin. She took a few steps over to her buckskin which was tethered beside Thad's chestnut, and wrapped her arms around the horse's neck.

'Father gave me this horse two years ago for my sixteenth birthday,' there was a sad wistfulness in her voice.

'It's a fine animal,' Thad replied.

'Yes.' Amanda patted the buckskin a few times. Her eyes appeared distant as she made her way back to the front door of the cabin where Thad was still standing. 'Sixteen, that's the age I was when Father told me the legend of Jimmy Ellis.'

'From what I can make out, it's a legend people don't want to talk about.'

'You can't blame them.' The woman paused. She seemed to be struggling with what to say next. She settled for, 'Let's walk over to the cottonwood.'

Thad walked beside Amanda as she moved slowly and

spoke in a low voice. 'A lot happened to our family when I was sixteen, most of it bad. My mother died very unexpectedly.'

'I'm sorry.'

'Thank you. Of course, it was hard on all of us, but Father in particular. He changed in many ways. He became . . . well . . . more religious.'

'That's not too surprising.'

'Perhaps, but in my father's case it's a bit odd. In the past, he hadn't cared much for church, but attended now and then with me and Mom to make Mother happy. Now, he goes every week. Seems to be his way of keeping Mom alive.'

They stopped at the cottonwood. Amanda gazed at the tree as if it were a religious shrine. 'A few months after Mom died, Father came home from church deeply troubled over something Reverend Davis said in his sermon. Don't know exactly what it was, but he had preached about people who try to hide their sins. After dinner, Father took me into his office and told me about Jimmy Ellis.'

'Who was Jimmy Ellis, anyhow?'

'A cold-blooded killer. Twenty years ago, he shot down a man named Fred Hawkins because Hawkins called him "sawbuck". That was a nickname Beau Haney had given Ellis when he was the sheriff of Tin Cup.'

'Did Haney arrest Jimmy Ellis?'

'No. Ellis dropped a half dollar piece on Fred Hawkins's corpse and rode out of Tin Cup fast. The law couldn't catch up with him.'

'So, what happened next?'

'About a week later, it was on a Saturday night, Ellis snuck back into town and broke into the home of Fred Hawkins's brother, Ralph. He killed the whole family: Ralph, his three kids all under the age of nine, and Ralph's wife.'

'I suppose he left behind his calling card, a sawbuck.'

'Yes.' Amanda reached up and broke off a long twig that protruded from one of the thick branches of the cottonwood. Her hands busied themselves pulling leaves off the twig as she continued. 'Father was playing cards in town at the time, along with some other ranchers. They joined the posse that rode out after Jimmy Ellis.'

Thad looked intently at the young woman who was staring at the remaining leaves on the twig. The deputy experienced a stirring inside him and wondered if Amanda might be feeling something similar. He tried to keep his mind on his duty. 'Must have been tough, tracking Ellis at night.'

'No. This time, the law got lucky. Beau Haney and his deputy Harry Clausen were doing a round when they heard the shots coming from the Hawkins house. There was a bright moon that night. Mr Clausen spotted Ellis riding off as he and Beau Haney entered the house and found five dead bodies. Mr Clausen took off after the killer while the sheriff got up a posse.'

'Harry Clausen could have left some obvious markers for the posse—'

Amanda looked up from the twig, and nodded her head. 'He even fired his gun a few times. Sheriff Haney and the posse had no trouble following him.' Using the twig as a pointer, she indicated the line shack. 'It all ended up with Jimmy Ellis in the shack and the posse on the hill trying to move in.'

'What happened?'

'Jimmy Ellis took a bullet in the shoulder. He threw out his gun and surrendered. Of course, it should have stopped right there, but it didn't.'

Night had now mastered the sky. A bright three-quarter

moon was surrounded by a gang of stars. Amanda tossed the twig to the ground as if she suddenly found it repellant.

'You have to remember, Mr Brookshire, Jimmy Ellis had killed six people including a woman and three children. Every man who went after the killer wanted vengeance. The posse hung Jimmy Ellis from this cottonwood.'

Thad was stunned, but kept his emotions in check. He wouldn't be helping anybody by denouncing a hanging that had taken place twenty years before. 'You mean, Sheriff Haney allowed it?'

Amanda's answer was quick. 'Yes. According to Father, Beau Haney resisted at first, but the men in the posse rawhided him. Haney was afraid of losing the respect of the townsmen. So, he went along with it.'

Thad shook his head. 'I can't believe Harry Clausen would stand by while a man was hung!'

Amanda was quick again. 'He didn't.'

'What do you mean?'

'Mr Clausen tried to talk the posse out of what they were about to do. When the men ignored him, Mr Clausen started to go for his gun. Beau Haney punched his own deputy . . . hard . . . knocked him down, then they tied him up.'

'It must have been awful.'

The young woman nodded her head. 'Father says Mr Clausen yelled at the posse to stop. Told them they would hate themselves for what they were doing. Then, Jimmy Ellis yelled at them as they put the noose around his neck.'

'What was he saying?'

'He told all the men they had better leave town. He would come back in twenty years and kill all of them who were still living in Tin Cup, except for Harry Clausen.'

'Did your father tell you how many men from that posse,

besides himself, are still living in town?'

Amanda nodded her head. 'There is Beau Haney. Art Sherman, he's a rancher around here, and Peter Kyle. Mr Kyle used to be a bartender; now he owns the Gold Coin. Of course there was Jed Coogan. Last and certainly not least is Clarence Newton.'

'The banker?'

'Yes. At the time, the Community Bank was less than a year old. Ellis was lynched by a mob that included the town banker as well as the sheriff.'

Thad tried to be delicate. 'I know Mr Haney has problems—'

'Beau Haney is a drunk!' Amanda was in no mood to be delicate. 'Father tells me he took to the bottle right after Jimmy Ellis was hung. Harry Clausen took over as sheriff about six months later.'

'Sheriff Clausen told me that Haney does odd jobs around town.'

'Yes, and the men who were in the posse give him money now and then. They feel responsible for what has happened to him. Father calls it blood money. Father's had nightmares about the hanging for the last twenty years. He can't shake off the horrible memory.'

Amanda stopped speaking and Thad could think of no more questions. The total silence made him jittery. There wasn't even the sound of a bird or wild animal: this was the silence of death.

He was relieved when the young woman spoke to him, her voice once again pleading. 'I felt I had to tell you about all this. You're new in town. I was afraid no one would tell you the whole story.'

'I'm sure Sheriff Clausen would have filled me in.'

Amanda spoke as if Thad hadn't said anything. 'And . . .

well . . . you're young and maybe your mind is sort of more open than other people.'

The deputy wondered where this was leading. 'I always try to keep an open mind.'

The young woman continued, 'Earlier today, when Leo Jensen came in with news about finding the body, I rode out with Father and Leo. I didn't want to look at the body. So, I walked around while Leo wrapped it in a blanket and put it in a wagon. I spotted something unusual. You see, Father told me they buried Jimmy Ellis around here in an unmarked grave, but he couldn't remember where.'

'You located the grave?'

Amanda motioned with an index finger for Thad to follow her. They walked past the cottonwood, to the far side of the cabin and a couple of yards behind it. Amanda pointed downward to where a hole and a wide scattering of dirt lay in front of a large boulder.

Thad crouched and examined the ripped ground. 'This hole was dug lately. It's about the size of a man.' He looked up at his companion. 'Do you think someone dug up the grave of Jimmy Ellis?'

Amanda pressed her lips together and glanced at the stars for a moment. A look of confusion came over her face as if something up there troubled her. 'Look at the loose dirt, what do you see?'

Thad shrugged his shoulders. 'The stuff is scattered all over the place.'

Amanda stared severely at the deputy and spoke like a schoolmarm addressing a child. 'When men dig a hole, they throw the dirt in the same place afterwards, making a mound.'

The deputy caught the implication. 'Hold on!' Thad sprung up and looked at the young woman. 'Are you saying

Jimmy Ellis came back to life and clawed his way out of the grave?'

A couple of tears loosened from the girl's eyes. 'I don't know. I was hoping you'd at least try to understand. . . .'

Thad felt angry with himself. Scoffing at a girl was no way to make a good impression on her and he wanted to make a good impression. 'Look, I'm sorry—'

As Thad began to approach Amanda, a gunshot spewed a cloud of dirt over his shoes. Amanda screamed as the deputy placed an arm around her.

'This way!' He pointed at the boulder.

Going into a jackknife position, the couple scurried behind the large rock as another shot pinged off it. 'Get down!' Brookshire yelled as he drew his gun. The woman knelt as Thad peeked over the boulder, trying to spot any sign of their attacker.

A flame blossomed from the other side of the shack. Brookshire ducked down and then sent a shot in that direction.

A harsh laugh filled the air. 'You can't kill a dead man!' The pounding of a horse's hoofs followed. Thad and Amanda both watched as a horse galloped up to the top of the hill. The rider was obviously a superb horseman and wearing a hat and duster. From the distance they could tell nothing else about him.

The strange figure stopped at the top of the hill, brought his horse up on two legs and fired a shot into the air. He laughed once more as he and his steed vanished on to the other side of the hill.

Amanda grabbed her companion's arm. 'We have to get to my father. He's alone and that . . . phantom . . . is on the loose, he could be heading for our ranch right now.'

'We have to be careful.' Thad pointed at the hill. 'He may

be hiding up there.'

Still holding his gun, Thad took Amanda's hand. Cautiously at first, then with increasing speed the couple stepped out from behind the boulder and moved briskly towards their horses. Thad let go of Amanda when they reached their steeds. The young woman mounted her buckskin and then gave a shriek.

'What is it, Miss Shaw?' Thad was now settled on to his chestnut.

'This was tied to my saddle horn.' She tossed a round object at the lawman.

Thad knew the object was a sawbuck before catching it.

'Let's ride,' he said.

CHAPTER SEVEN

As they rode up the steep hill and down the other side, Thad noted that his companion was better on a horse than he was. The discovery didn't bother him. Amanda's life on a ranch had provided far more experience with horses than his life in Dallas had. That was now changing.

Off the hill, both Amanda and Thad spurred their horses into a fast gallop. The deputy marveled at the strange excitement that coursed through him. Yes, he cared about rescuing Abner Shaw, but it went beyond that.

Amanda's hair fluttered in the wind as she bent forward on her buckskin. Ribbons of dust flowed from under the horse's hoofs. Increasingly, Thad felt himself in a glorious rhythm with his own horse, now stretched out, as he drew alongside Amanda.

The two young people exchanged quick smiles. They were two people on a vital mission, working together.

Amanda motioned to him that they would soon be turning off on to another trail. Thad allowed the woman to pull ahead of him and followed as she veered leftward. A large tree lay across the path, its branches propping the trunk up by about six feet. Amanda's buckskin seemed to make the jump effortlessly. Thad held his breath and closed his eyes as the chestnut followed the actions of the buckskin, landing smoothly and not pausing as it resumed its gallop.

A giddiness came over Thad as he regained his position beside Amanda. This was the only kind of life a man should ever want!

His giddiness subsided as they neared the ranch. Amanda pulled up on her buckskin. The moment the horse had completely stopped, she stood up in the saddle.

Thad reined in beside her. They were now directly facing the main ranch house. Thad saw the worried look on Amanda's face. He spoke in a whisper, 'What is it?'

'I thought I saw someone run behind the house, could be wrong but. . . .'

The lawman dismounted. 'You stay here.'

Thad ran to the wooden fence that surrounded the house. The gate opened easily. Light beamed from the front window, but Thad couldn't spot any people inside. He moved quickly but quietly around the house to the back. No lights shone from the back windows. The lawman figured the trees that ran along the fence provided welcome shade during the day, but now only provided more darkness for a killer to take refuge.

A sharp clang spiked against the night. The deputy could

see the outline of a tool shed, about twenty yards away. His prey had probably sought refuge in the shed only to knock over a pick or shovel.

Thad drew his gun, moved towards the extra darkness near the fence, and advanced on the shed. The structure was perched about halfway between the back corners of the fence and away from the shade of the trees. The lawman reckoned he was finally having some luck: moonlight would silhouette the killer if he tried to run off.

When he was only a few feet away from the tool shed, Thad moved from the shadows and stood directly in front of the structure's door. Moonlight confirmed his earlier assumption that the wooden structure had no windows. 'I know you're in there. Throw out your gun and come out with your hands up.'

Nothing happened. The deputy thought about shouting another order, but decided against it. He stepped gingerly toward the shed. Of course, the killer knew he was coming, but there was no sense in making a formal announcement.

Thad pressed his body against the shed, directly beside the doorknob. His own breathing sounded loud to him as did the surrounding noises. From a bunkhouse came the discordant noises of men both arguing and laughing over a poker game. Further away a coyote howled. Smaller varmints rustled in the trees.

Thad turned the knob and flung open the door. He was greeted by a dark cavity. As his eyes began to make out a row of shovels lined against a far wall, the deputy realized he didn't know what to do next. Should he step inside or. . .

The deputy heard a swooshing sound before he felt the sharp pain that knocked him into near unconsciousness. Thad dropped his gun, collided with the door and then went down on his knees, partially from the force of the blow and partially in search of the weapon. His hand found the .44. He crawled a few steps and tried to get up but was stopped by a hard kick to his back. Thad's face collided with the ground.

A woman's scream cut the night and seemed to stop everything. The friendly ruckus from the bunkhouse ceased and even the animals went still.

'Are you OK?' Amanda crouched over the deputy, but was immediately yanked away. This time, the woman's attempt at a scream was cut off by an arm that clamped around her neck in a vice-like hold.

The lawman quickly picked himself up, .44 still in hand. His vision was wavy, but he could still see Amanda being held by a figure wearing a duster and a hat pulled down low. The moon reflected off the revolver in his hand, flickering like a dying lantern flame.

'Throw down the gun, deputy!' The orders were accompanied by Amanda's gasps. Her windpipe was almost closed by the grip that enclosed it.

'Let the girl go!' Thad shouted.

'Throw down the gun, deputy, throw it far away, or this girlie gets a bullet in her head.'

Thad followed the orders. Pounding steps of men running towards the ranch house sounded from not far off. The captor released Amanda. The woman took a deep breath, then shrieked in pain as the masked figure slammed his free hand against the back of her neck.

Amanda collapsed. Thad ran to the woman as her former captor vanished into the surrounding darkness.

The deputy crouched beside Amanda; she was again breathing deeply. 'Are you OK?'

Amanda smiled, 'I just asked you the same question.'

*

A large number of people milled about in the living room of the Rocking S Ranch. Leo Jensen, the ramrod, was speaking to Abner Shaw, who sat in the room's largest chair.

'The men were either in the bunkhouse, Mr Shaw, or near it, when we heard Miss Shaw scream. Of course, we all came running. First, we came in here and found you with the rifle, getting ready to run out back.'

'Yes, I had trouble finding it. Don't know why. The Henry was where I always keep it.'

Thad felt sorry for Abner Shaw. The man appeared to be very old, probably older than he actually was. The owner of the Rocking S was trying to project authority. He wanted to be viewed as a man in command. He came across more as a figure of pity.

Jensen continued. 'George, Cal, me and a few others ran outside. We found Miss Shaw with Thad Brookshire. That's when Miss Shaw told us about the ghost of Jimmy Ellis.'

'That wasn't any ghost that hit me out there, tonight!' Thad spoke from a small sofa where he sat with Amanda. Since both had been injured, Abner had insisted they sit down.

Jensen looked at the ranch hands who were standing around nervously shifting their weight from one foot to the next. 'Ghost or no ghost, whoever was out there tonight was too fast and too smart for the Lightning Kid!'

Guffaws filled the room, stopped by the anxious look on Abner Shaw's face. Thad understood the ramrod's hostility. Jensen wanted Amanda for his own and viewed him as a threat.

The deputy addressed his words to Abner Shaw as he stood up. 'There's nothing more I can do here tonight. Soon as I get back to town, I'll—'

Amanda bolted up. 'No, Thad. Father and I won't hear of

it. You've got to stay here tonight. You shouldn't ride so soon.'

'But I need to do an early morning round tomorrow.'

'You can leave early. After you've had a good rest. I insist.'

Thad saw several ranch hands turn their faces to the floor, trying to hide their smirks. Leo Jensen didn't look down. He stared at the lawman with raw hatred.

CHAPTER EIGHT

Harry Clausen pulled at his mustache and tried to think of the right thing to say. His new deputy had made a passel of mistakes last night and the sheriff knew why. Thad Brookshire had been smitten by Amanda Shaw.

Clausen didn't blame the kid. Amanda could knock the common sense out of any man. Still, the deputy who now sat in front of his desk looking sheepish needed to be set straight.

Harry decided that a businesslike approach was called for. 'Now, when you arrived at the ranch and thought that . . . ah. . . .' The sheriff had started to say, 'Jimmy Ellis,' but checked himself. 'You thought the jasper who fired on you at the shack could be on the ranch. Why didn't you ask Miss Shaw to alert the ranch hands? They could have surrounded the area.'

Thad inhaled and exhaled nervously. 'I didn't think of it, sir.'

The sheriff felt uncomfortable. He didn't get called 'sir'

very much. He softened his voice. 'After you got Miss Shaw into the ranch house and saw that she and her father were safe, you shoulda looked over the grounds. The prowler might have left foot prints or dropped somethin'.'

'I'm sorry, sir. I really am.'

'I know you are.' Harry folded his hands in front of him and leaned closer to his deputy, emphasizing the importance of his next point. 'Next time, tell me when somethin' like this comes up. There can't be any secrets between lawmen.'

Thad smiled and nodded his head. A silent understanding passed between the two men. Harry felt both good and a bit awkward. He reckoned men who had sons went through this sort of thing a lot and wondered why, in the past, he couldn't have met some fine gal and . . .

The sheriff thought it a good thing when Rance Dehner entered the office. Harry Clausen was starting to feel sorry for himself. No sense in that, he thought. Harry had already explained Rance's status as a volunteer deputy to Thad. Now, he could go over Thad's adventures from the previous evening with Dehner.

A brief silence followed the sheriff's explanations. Rance broke it as he spoke in an almost jocular voice. 'Gentlemen, I think we need to call a meeting!'

'A meeting of whom?' Harry got up from his desk and moved towards the coffee pot that sat on a pot-bellied stove. Thad made his way to the gun rack that hung on a side wall of the office, directly across from the stove. The rifles needed to be cleaned.

'A meeting of everyone who served in that posse twenty years ago. Those men could be in danger. Their families too.'

'Their families?' The sheriff stopped before reaching the stove.

'Twenty years ago, Jimmy Ellis killed the family of a man who insulted him,' Dehner explained. 'Whoever wants us to think he is Jimmy Ellis may try to pull a similar stunt.'

'Hadn't thought of that!' Thad slowly took a Winchester down from the rack. 'Amanda could be in danger . . . ah . . . along with the rest of the families.'

Clausen gave up on the coffee. 'You two gents will hafta watch after the town for a spell.'

'Where are you going?' Thad asked.

The sheriff picked his Stetson up off of his desk. 'Gotta see Art Sherman and Abner Shaw. I'm ridin' out to their places. We need to have that meetin' soon.' He opened the door and gave Dehner a quick glance. 'Could you talk to Peter Kyle over at the Gold Coin and Clarence Newton the banker? Tell them to be in this office at seven tonight. Don't let 'em say no.'

'Sure. How about Beau Haney?'

'Him too. Beau don't need much advance notice. He doesn't have a very busy schedule these days.' Clausen put on his hat and slammed the door shut as he left.

The rest of the morning passed uneventfully. Shortly after noon, Dirk Beecher, who owned the Beecher Hotel, stormed into the office. 'I gotta see Sheriff Clausen!'

'He's not here right now, Mr Beecher,' Rance was staying at the hotel and recognized the man. 'We're his deputies, can we help?'

Dehner had hoped his soft voice would calm the hotel owner. It didn't work. Beecher continued to shout, 'You've got to come right away!'

'Sure.' Dehner said crisply. He and Thad Brookshire followed the hotel owner out of the office and north on the boardwalk towards the hotel.

'What exactly is the problem, Mr Beecher?' Thad asked.

'Some no good drifter came into the hotel about two hours ago. He ate a big meal in the hotel's restaurant, and refused to pay his bill. The restaurant manager came to get me. I was doin' some work on the second floor at the time. When we got back downstairs, we found the no-good lyin' on a sofa in the lobby dead asleep.'

As they entered the hotel, Dirk Beecher paraded directly to the sofa and pointed at the snoring object spread sloppily over it. 'That man is lowerin' the tone of the hotel!'

'You've got a point,' Dehner said as he looked down at the obese, unshaven man who lay on the sofa. Saliva leaked from his open mouth and he smelled like he had last taken a bath on Christmas Day. It was now September.

The job was slow and unpleasant, but Rance and Thad managed to rouse the saddle tramp and get him on to his feet. He had enough money in his pockets to pay about half of his restaurant bill. That satisfied Dirk Beecher who wanted the trouble gone.

'What are you doing in Tin Cup?' Rance asked the drifter.

'Jus' passin' through,' came the bleary-eyed response.

Rance pointed at Thad and then at himself. 'We'll help you pass through.'

The two deputies accompanied the tramp out of the hotel and on to his horse. 'We didn't exactly apprehend the James gang,' Dehner spoke to Thad as they watched the drifter ride slowly out of town. 'But this sort of thing is a big part of a lawman's job.'

'Guess I'd better get used to it,' Thad replied.

Dehner ran Thad's response over in his mind as they walked back to the sheriff's office. The detective still thought he needed to hold off on telling the young man about his father. Thad Brookshire was at an important crossroads in his life. He needed to ride out the Jimmy Ellis matter. Then, he could return home to his family, either to stay in Dallas and or just for a visit before he returned to a life as a lawman.

As the two men drew near the office, they spotted a woman peering into the front window. Only a few more steps were needed to peg the woman as Amanda Shaw.

Thad's footsteps quickened. His back was to Dehner when he spoke to Amanda. 'Good afternoon, Miss Shaw.'

'Good afternoon, Mr Brookshire. I couldn't sleep last night what with all that happened.' She lifted up a round object in her hands. 'So, I baked a pie for you and Sheriff Clausen . . . and for you, Mr . . .'

'Dehner.' The detective touched two fingers to his flat crowned hat as he unlocked the office door.

Amanda apologized for forgetting Rance's name as the threesome entered the office. Thad began to joke about eating all the pie himself. The laughter was forced and Dehner realized that his presence was not helping matters.

'That pie sure looks good.' Dehner spoke as Amanda placed the treasure on the sheriff's desk and briefly lifted one of the towels it was wrapped in. 'But we should wait until Sheriff Clausen gets back before we cut it. Meanwhile, why don't you two go have lunch?'

Rance could tell from the expression on both of their faces that he had made an excellent suggestion, but Thad felt obligated to offer a token resistance.

'I hate to leave you here with—'

'No trouble at all. I'll grab a bite when you get back. Now, get out of here!'

Thad felt nervous as he walked with Amanda to Corry's Café. There was a question he wanted to ask her, but was afraid he might be rushing things. The girl might say, 'no.' Then what would he do?

They were seated in the café and had ordered their lunch when Amanda's expression clouded up with worry. 'Are you OK, Mr Brookshire?'

'Yes, I'm fine.'

'Oh . . . that's good.'

'Miss Shaw, you and I haven't known each other very long. But we've already been through a lot together.'

Amanda smiled and nodded her head. 'Yes.'

'I was wondering,' Thad inhaled deeply before continuing in a fast voice, 'Could I call you by your first name? I'd be honored if you'd call me Thad.'

Amanda rubbed a finger on the checkered table cloth. 'Why, thank you, and yes, Mr Brook— I mean, Thad, I think that would be nice.'

At that point, the conversation became very happy and effusive. Thad's lawman's instincts were still sprouting. He didn't even notice the stranger who swaggered into the café. The couple's happy moment was about to be shattered.

CHAPTER NINE

'So, you're the Lightnin' Kid!' The stranger's voice was loud and sharp. 'They got half of it right. You ain't no man, just a kid.'

Thad was still feeling giddy in the presence of Amanda Shaw. He didn't hear the stranger clearly and had missed the threat in his voice.

'I'm not the Lightning Kid anymore.' He looked up and

smiled at the stranger, who was now leaning on a counter at the back of the café. 'I'm Deputy Thad Brookshire, just call me—'

'That piece of tin don't mean nothin' to me. I got a little argument to settle with you, Lightnin' Kid.'

Amanda placed a hand on the lawman's arm. 'Thad, let's leave, right now.'

The newcomer gave a harsh, theatrical laugh. 'Seems the Lightnin' Kid needs to hide behind a girlie.'

Thad stood up. 'I don't intend to argue. You don't seem very happy here, stranger. Leave town. Now. No arguments.'

Amanda ran from the café. At 1.30 in the afternoon, most of the lunch crowd had gone. Hugh Corry scurried out from the kitchen and quickly escorted an elderly couple, who were now the only customers besides Thad and the man who was taunting him, out the door and on to the boardwalk. From there, they watched through the café's window.

'Everbody's left. Even the girlie. Must be because they got offended by your rude behavior, Lightnin' Kid. Why, you didn't even ask my name.'

Thad decided to play along. Maybe this could be settled without a gunfight. But he couldn't appear weak. A mocking tone entered the deputy's voice. 'Pardon me! What's your name?'

'Stan Carmody, ever hear of me?'

The laughter that came from Thad was genuine. 'Sure have. I read an article about you in an old issue of that fool magazine that wrote about me, written by the same crazy jasper, Foster Lewis. He tagged you, "Red Lightning". I'm sure he lied about you, just as he lied about me.'

Carmody pushed his hat back revealing a lock of red hair. He stepped away from the counter. His right hand hovered over the six shooter in his holster. 'Nothin' said about the speed of Red Lightnin' is a lie. I suspect he lied plenty 'bout you, cause you tole him lies. Well, I ain't gonna share the name of "Lightnin' " with no liar.'

Thad stood flabbergasted. He stared intently at the outlaw who now stood parallel to him and about fifteen feet away. 'You'd risk death and maybe kill a man over a silly name!'

'That's right, junior. I'm gonna kill you right—'

'Hello, Stan.' Rance Dehner stepped into the restaurant and moved laconically around the empty tables and chairs. 'Been a while since our trails crossed. What, about sixteen months?'

Carmody was not happy to see Dehner, but tried to sound casual. 'Yep, somethin' like that.'

Rance maintained his mock friendliness. 'How'd that range war up north go? As I recall, you were a gunney for the Bar H outfit.'

'It went real good,' Carmody snapped his reply. 'The Bar H got just what it wanted.'

Rance eyed the gunfighter carefully. Stan Carmody had changed since Dehner last saw him. A patch of veins had settled on to his nose and a roll of flesh hung over his belt. His eyes beamed desperation.

'That's not exactly the case, Stan,' Dehner smiled broadly. 'You left one very important detail out.'

'What's that?'

Dehner stepped casually in front of the deputy and motioned for him to stay where he was. 'From what I hear, the rancher opposing the Bar H hired some fast guns. Men with reputations better than yours. You demanded money up front from the owner of the Bar H, but when the showdown came, Stan Carmody couldn't be found.'

'That's a lie!'

'I don't think it's a lie, Carmody.' A look of understanding fell over Thad's face as he spoke. 'You're trying the same trick again, only you have to puff up your reputation first. That magazine lied about you, so you figured it lied about me, too. You want to kill the Lightning Kid. After that, you'll collect money from another rancher caught up in a range war and run out on him.'

Carmody shouted angry curses at the deputy. Rance took a few steps toward the counter and turned to face the gunney with his right hand positioned over his Colt .45. He needed to focus Carmody's attention on himself.

'How many men have you killed, Stan?' Dehner asked.

Carmody's eyes darted sideways. A crowd was now watching from the window. He couldn't back down.

'Nine!' The gunman shouted.

Dehner smirked before speaking. 'I suppose you're anxious to move into the double digits.'

Laughter could be heard from outside. Carmody knew they were laughing at him. He had to act fast. 'I can kill you anytime I want, Dehner.'

'Prove it.'

Stan Carmody was fighting for his life and reputation, to him they were the same thing. He shrugged his shoulders and looked at the floor. 'Maybe we both need to cool off, Rance. No need for anyone to get hurt. How 'bout I buy you a drink—'

That old trick had worked for Carmody before, but not this time. The gunfighter had cleared leather and started to lift his weapon when a horrible burn speared through his leg. The leg became hot rubber and Carmody plunged to the floor, still clutching his gun.

One good shot was all he needed. The gunfighter's vision was now blurred but he started to aim his six shooter in the direction of his opponent. Dehner's boot slammed into his hand and the gun skidded across the floor until it bumped against a wall.

Cheering sounded from outside. Amanda stormed into the café and embraced Thad. 'Please don't think I ran out on you. I went to get Mr Dehner, I didn't want you to—'

Thad didn't say anything. He was content to have his arms around the girl.

Hugh Corry was right behind Amanda. He sped over to where Dehner stood over Stan Carmody. Rance was saying something to the gunman, but Corry wasn't interested. He took a quick look at the fallen gunslinger. Sounds of panic came from Hugh's throat as he made his way hurriedly behind the counter and ran back to Dehner with several towels in his hand.

'I gotta get these things under his leg,' Hugh shouted as he held up the towels. 'Blood stains is really hard to get outta wood.'

Carmody gave a loud bellow as the café owner yanked up his leg and placed towels on the floor to absorb the blood.

'Plenty of men still outside,' Hugh spoke as he glanced out the window. 'I'll get some help. We'll carry this owlhoot over to the doc's. Get him outta here.'

Hugh ran off on his mission. Rance resumed his talk with Carmody. 'As soon as the doc is finished with you, you're leaving town for good. Understand?'

Stan Carmody's voice was whispery. 'I'll be happy to leave this. . . .'

A string of curses followed. Dehner retrieved the gunman's weapon, then walked over to Amanda and Thad. The couple was no longer embracing. They both seemed uneasy over their public display of affection.

'Thanks for what you did, Rance, ' Thad said. 'But you

didn't have to. . . .'

Rance understood the situation and didn't want the young man to feel diminished in the eyes of a woman he obviously wanted very much to impress. Truth was the best remedy for that.

'You could have taken Stan Carmody, but I didn't want you to.'

'Why not?' Thad asked.

The answer was delayed by a barrage of frantic noise as Hugh Corry returned with four volunteers and a crude stretcher. Carmody bellowed even louder than before as they placed him on the contraption and carried him out.

Dehner smiled at his companions. 'I guess Hugh won't have to worry any more about blood stains on his floor.'

The detective pushed back his hat: time to answer Thad's question. 'You've already killed one man. I didn't want you to kill another. I've had more experience. I thought I could bring down Carmody without killing him.'

Thad nodded his head somberly. 'I understand.'

'There's one more thing you need to understand,' Dehner shot back.

'What's that?'

There was now not even a touch of a smile on Dehner's face. His eyes were hard. 'Don't try what I did today. Not for a long time. When you shoot, shoot to kill.'

CHAPTER TEN

Harry Clausen looked at the men seated around his desk and tried not to think about what they all looked like twenty years back. Time had been kind to some of them, not so kind to others.

Beau Haney had been a respected lawman, but he had betrayed his calling and now was paying a terrible price. Abner Shaw was a good man who could never forgive himself for helping to lynch Jimmy Ellis. But Abner had managed to get on with his life, until lately. Harry thought about what the preacher had said about Abner Shaw: 'His soul seems to be draining out of him.' Yup, that pretty much said it. Amanda had pleaded with her father to hand over responsibilities for the ranch to someone else, but so far Abner had remained stubbornly in charge.

The other men had done well and had left the Jimmy Ellis matter behind. Art Sherman's ranch was prosperous. Peter Kyle owned the Gold Coin, Tin Cup's most popular saloon. And the town couldn't survive without Clarence Newton's bank. Clarence was probably the most important man in town.

Of course, the most important man in town had blood on his hands, but folks didn't talk about that much.

Harry sat at his desk with Thad Brookshire seated on his left and Dehner on his right. The sheriff was nervous and hoped it didn't show. 'Thanks for comin' here tonight, gents. This won't take long. I promised Reverend Davis I'd get these extra chairs back to him tonight. I took 'em right outta the school house.'

Uneasy laughter bounced between the men as they all tried to appear casual.

Clausen warned the men that whoever was posing as the ghost of Jimmy Ellis might try to harm their families. 'Art, you've got your wife to think of and I know those two boys of yours are gettin' big, but warn 'em anyhow. Young folks, especially the male kind, tend not to be very careful.'

Art Sherman nodded his head politely. There was a touch of condescension in the movement as if he were placating a fussy relative. Sherman was a large, muscular man, totally bald and slightly overweight. In Harry Clausen's opinion, Sherman never paid attention to anything people said, but the sheriff believed he had to try.

Clausen lowered his voice. He felt very awkward. 'Peter, of course I know you're a widower and your daughter has moved East,' Harry tried to inject a touch of levity into his voice, 'so I reckon you only got yourself to worry about.'

Rance thought he noticed a look of understanding pass between Peter Klye and Harry Clausen: the loneliness of two men who had their jobs to live for and little else. Kyle pulled at his handlebar mustache, but said nothing.

The sheriff quickly turned his attention to Clarence Newton. 'You've got a heap of folks that need protectin'. Whoever is tryin' to convince us he's Jimmy Ellis could try doin' some harm to those grandkids of yours, or the rest of the family.'

'Thank you Sheriff, I will take suitable precautions.' The banker sounded calm and businesslike, but then, Clausen reckoned, Newton always sounded calm and businesslike. The banker had iron grey hair, stooped shoulders and seemed always to be fussing with a pipe. Harry mused that the banker had even been puffing on a pipe when. . . .

The sheriff tried again not to think about the past. He spoke softly to Abner Shaw and then talked to Beau Haney, who was already well on his way to being drunk. Beau had no family and Clausen wondered if death wouldn't be a mercy for the former lawman.

Harry leaned forward and continued with his warnings. 'All of you men need to keep in mind that I'm jus' one old lawdog with a force of two deputies. You gents are gonna hafta look after your families and make sure they're safe.'

'Is that all, Sheriff?' Sherman's voice was loud and belligerent.

'Pardon?' Clausen didn't try to hide his irritation.

Art Sherman looked amused. 'If you have nothing else to say, then we'll be going and you and your deputies can carry these chairs back to the school house.'

'Well, as a matter of fact, Art, there is somethin' else I need to say before you can return to your important schedule!'

Harry Clausen breathed deeply and tried to reign in his temper. Art Sherman continued to appear amused, which didn't help the sheriff any.

When Harry spoke again, he tried to duplicate the banker's business-like voice. 'We all know the main thing you gents have in common: you lynched Jimmy Ellis. Now, rememberin' that this here meetin' is confidential, I need to know if there's anythin' else you gents have in common. Is there any other thread between you?'

A nervous tension suddenly fell over the group. Even Art Sherman twitched in his chair.

Clarence Newton took the pipe out of his mouth and began to examine it. 'Well, yes, Sheriff Clausen, there is one thing.'

'And what's that, Clarence?'

'There is something in common between all of these men,' He pointed his pipe at Beau Haney. 'Except for Beau.'

Impatience crept into the sheriff's voice. 'I'm listenin'!'

Newton raised his pipe as if he were returning it to his mouth, but then hastily lowered it. 'The bank currently holds post-dated cheques signed by Art Sherman, Abner Shaw and Peter Kyle. These three gentlemen play poker together occasionally and I suspect each knows that the others have postdated cheques at the bank, though each transaction was made separately.'

The three gentlemen Clarence had just mentioned all nodded their heads.

'Why would a bank accept post-dated cheques?' Thad asked.

'It's a very common practice, young man!' Clarence snapped. 'At least it is in a ranching town. A rancher makes money at a certain time of year and not before. The bank can, officially, only loan him so much money. Accepting a post-dated cheque is, in effect, an additional loan. Ranchers couldn't survive without it.'

Thad still looked confused. 'But Mr Kyle—'

'Peter Kyle recently bought out his competitor,' Newton's voice now became angry. 'The bank loaned him money for the purchase, but. . . .'

'Family problems meant the owner of the Paradise Saloon needed to move back East fast,' Kyle explained. 'I didn't have enough money on hand to buy the Paradise. My head bartender, Otto, agreed on a partnership. He gets one quarter of the profits from the Paradise and the Gold Coin, but otherwise works for nothing. Even so, I needed a regular bank loan and I needed Clarence to accept a post-dated cheque, so I could purchase the Paradise.'

Dehner listened carefully, but said nothing. He suspected

that Clarence's anger had nothing to do with Thad's questions. The banker was withholding information and it made him nervous.

The detective suspected Clarence didn't want to discuss Abner Shaw's post-dated cheque. It was probably for a smaller amount than the others. Dehner had jawed with Clarence about the Rocking S. The banker had been discreet, but Rance understood that Abner could lose his ranch.

Sheriff Clausen talked for a few more minutes and managed to bring the meeting to a civil conclusion if not exactly a pleasant one. The three lawmen remained in the office as the others departed.

Once Art and his colleagues were outside the office, the rancher shouted in a jovial voice, 'Why don't all of us murderers of Jimmy Ellis retire to the Gold Coin for a few drinks? What a wonderful sign of our continuing camaraderie.'

Abner Shaw lifted a trembling hand. 'I gotta get over to the stable. Leo Jensen is waitin' there. He and Stanley are playin' checkers. Leo came into town with me.'

Sherman's smile and voice were contemptuous. 'Of course, Abner. We don't want you staying up past your bedtime.'

Abner Shaw nodded his head in a strange, sad gesture. The man seemed to be acknowledging that he could no longer fight back. Accepting insults without retribution was now a part of his life.

Abner began his slow walk to the livery. Art Sherman watched him without trying to rein in his laughter.

Clarence Newton pointed his pipe accusingly at Sherman. 'What's wrong with you? There is no need to treat Abner in such a cruel manner.'

'Well, look at Mr Righteous!' Sherman enjoyed shifting

his attention to the banker. 'The vulture who's waiting to foreclose on the Rocking S.'

Shock ignited in the banker's face. 'What do you know—'

'I know plenty! I've ridden over the Rocking S, I can spot a failing ranch.'

Newton fell silent. Sherman returned to his jovial voice. 'So, how about it, Clarence, want to join me for a drink?'

'No.'

'You don't drink much, do you Clarence?'

'No, Art, I don't.'

'I don't cotton to a man who doesn't drink.' Art Sherman turned to look at Peter Kyle and Beau Haney who were standing off together, staying out of the conversation. 'Sorry Peter, this little discussion has turned me downright unsociable.' He pointed at the former lawman. 'Guess you'll have to drink with your best customer.'

Sherman stepped off the boardwalk and walked across the street like a king leaving his entourage. Clarence watched with envy as the rancher untied his horse from a hitch rail and mounted. Art Sherman owns the finest horse in this county, the banker thought: a large black with identical white stockings on each leg.

Newton watched as Art Sherman rode off. He even moved to the centre of the street to watch the rancher depart. His envy was replaced by curiosity. Art Sherman was not riding towards his ranch.

Sherman didn't notice the banker's interest. He was too caught up in his private thoughts.

Only the strongest of men could prosper in the West, Sherman mused to himself. Most of the men in Tin Cup were survivors and nothing more. A few, like Beau Haney and Pop Cummings weren't even survivors. They lived off charity.

'Not Art Sherman,' the rancher whispered and then looked at the stars before continuing his thoughts. He had always been a man of great strength and always would be. He was a man who took what he wanted and if anybody got in his way . . . well . . . too bad for them.

Similar musings ran through Sherman's mind as he guided his horse to a familiar location. A broad smile cut across his face as he rode up the hill, paused at the top and gazed over the scene below. He laughed aloud and then spurred the black downwards.

At the bottom of the hill, Sherman dismounted beside the large cottonwood and didn't even bother to tether his horse. He stared at the tree which held such vital memories for him.

Yes, that night twenty years ago had been the time when Art Sherman showed his true power for the first time. The posse had carried Jimmy Ellis to the cottonwood, but then they began to lose their resolve. Beau Haney had started shouting about the law and a fair trial.

Sherman whispered to himself again. 'I backed Haney down.' He remembered how he had mocked the sheriff, questioned his manhood, and called him an old woman. By the time he was done with the lawman, Haney not only went along with the lynching, he landed a haymaker on his deputy when Harry Clausen tried to stop the mob.

The wealthy rancher continued to visualize that fateful night. Yes, he had been the one who slapped the horse that held Jimmy Ellis and he had cheered as the killer's legs kicked frantically about. The others turned their heads away, but not Art Sherman. He—'

'Good evening, Mr Sherman.'

The rancher turned around. Confusion filled his face and voice. 'I don't understand, what—'

'You don't have to understand, Mr Sherman.'

Four bullets ripped into Art Sherman. His body jerked backwards in a series of violent, convulsive motions. A buzzing sound filled his ears, but he could still hear the panicked hoof beats as his horse galloped off.

The rancher staggered around in a circle. He made a slight whistling sound, like an infant craving attention, before dropping to the ground on his back. Life was seeping out of Art Sherman fast. His vision was fuzzy and the buzzing grew louder. His final sight was a small object hurtling down at him from out of a vast blur. He suddenly realized it was a half dollar piece: a sawbuck. His eyes closed. The last moments of his life were spent listening to manic laughter that cut through the loud drone filling his head.

CHAPTER ELEVEN

Foster Lewis stepped into the Crystal Palace, one of Dallas's more expensive establishments. The large restaurant-saloon featured a stage where there was a floor show every night. Lewis hastily pulled out his pocket watch, only a few minutes past ten. Almost an hour before the last show would go on. Mitzi would still have time to talk to him.

The writer hastily glanced around the Crystal Palace which, as always, had a large crowd. He heard Mitzi's earthy laugh before he spotted her. She was squeezing the arm of one of the men engaged in a poker game.

'Ike, the way your luck is going, you'll own this place before the week is done.'

Ike laughed heartily. 'And when I do, Mitzi, I'll make you the star of the show!'

Boisterous laughter followed the remark and Mitzi gave everyone at the table a bright smile as she danced away. Foster watched that smile diminish as Mitzi spotted him walking towards her.

'Evening, Foster.' There was no music in her voice.

'Can we talk, Mitzi? Just for a few minutes.'

'You'll have to buy me a drink.'

'Sure.' He pointed toward an empty table. Mitzi signaled a waiter.

'I'm on to something big, Mitzi!' Foster spoke as they sat down.

The woman laughed harshly. 'What is it now?'

'A detective visited the magazine a few days ago.'

'Your boss is hiring someone to spy on his cheating wife.'

'It had nothing to do with the boss's wife. Remember that story I did on The Lightning Kid?'

'No.'

'The story was in our last issue.'

'I didn't read the last issue. Don't plan to read the current issue.'

'The detective was asking questions about the Kid, so after he left I did some detective work of my own.'

'How thrilling.' For the first time since she had sat down at the table, Mitzi smiled. The smile was for the waiter who delivered two drinks, a whiskey for Foster and a glass of water for Mitzi. Foster paid for both drinks. The waiter claimed, 'The lady is having vodka.' This came as no surprise to Lewis, he had suffered through this routine many times.

Foster waited until the waiter had left before continuing. 'The Lightning Kid is the son of a rich man, William Brookshire.'

The woman once again gave a joyless laugh. 'That's as close as you'll ever get to real money.'

Foster nervously caressed his mustache. 'I've got something big planned.'

'You always do.'

The writer leaned in toward Mitzi. 'The Lightning Kid is going to terrorize a poor family. Finally, one of the sons of that family will get fed up and challenge the Kid.'

'Of course, the poor boy will triumph over the rich no good.'

'Exactly!' Foster almost shouted. 'People love to read stuff like that. This could make a great book. I'll make hundreds, thousands. We can get married, move—'

'Foster, how long have we known each other?'

'About four years.'

The irritation in Mitzi's voice subsided replaced by a touch of sadness. 'When we first met, you were a reporter with the *Dallas Herald.* You were going to make me famous, then you got fired—'

'That wasn't my fault. . . .'

'I don't care anymore! Foster, I'm tired of your crazy dreams. If this Lightning Kid is going to make you wealthy, fine. But don't bother me again until you are rich.'

Mitzi got up, leaving her water untouched. Foster drank alone. He left the Crystal Palace with a fanatical determination that this time his scheme would work.

CHAPTER TWELVE

'As most of you know, I recently presided at the funeral of Art Sherman. Brother Sherman's family is here in church worshipping with us this morning. What a wonderful testimony of faith.'

There was a strong, respectful chorus of amens from the congregation, after which Reverend Levi Davis continued. 'This town is grieving over the murders of two of its beloved citizens. I will leave law enforcement to our outstanding sheriff and his fine deputies, but I'm convinced that a factor in these horrible killings is alcohol: the devil's brew, which corrupts the souls of men and robs them of their morality.'

There was another round of amens. Thad Brookshire from his position in a back pew noted with amusement that this time, the amens were slight and scattered. No surprise. Many of the men now sitting in the church beside their wives and kids could have been found last night bending their elbows at the Gold Coin.

Thad didn't really care. The sermon was no better nor worse than ones he had heard before. What mattered to the young man was the lady sitting beside him. Amanda Shaw looked more beautiful than ever in her Sunday clothes. Thad felt like he was already in Heaven.

Of course, Heaven on earth does have its limitations. Sitting on Amanda's other side was her father and beside him was Leo Jensen. Being in God's house did not diminish the harsh glares which Jensen frequently shot at the deputy.

'Tomorrow night, in this church, there will be a meeting

of the Temperance Union,' Reverend Davis continued. 'In concluding my sermon, I urge all of you to attend. I extend a special invitation to all of you men. In troubled times like these, our community needs men who aren't afraid to demonstrate some spiritual backbone!'

Thad noticed that the males in the congregation looked grateful for the final hymn when it arrived at last to close the service. Outside the church, as everyone stood around and chatted, Thad and Amanda were swamped with attention from the ladies. In Tin Cup, a young man and woman attending Sunday morning worship together was a significant statement.

Leo Jensen stood at Abner Shaw's side as he talked at length with the pastor. Jensen then accompanied Abner as he rejoined his daughter and her companion.

The old man smiled at Thad. 'Deputy, we'd be happy to have you as our guest for lunch. There is always room for one more at the Shaw table.'

Amanda looked a bit uneasy. 'Father, I thought I would stay here in town for the day. Thad has already invited me to lunch at the hotel restaurant, and he will see me safely to the evening service.'

Abner smiled wanly, 'Wish I could come back into town and attend the evening service. Just don't have the energy for it right now.'

There was nothing wan about the expression on Leo Jensen's face. 'Miss Shaw, you gotta go back with us.' Jensen cleared his throat, realizing that his statement had been too demanding. 'You can't ride a horse in such a fine dress. You need a buckboard.'

Amanda smiled at the ramrod. 'Thank you for your concern, Mr Jensen. But Thad has already rented a buggy from Stanley Abbot. I'm sure he will be able to get me back to the Rocking S without harming my dress.'

Jensen said nothing. Abner hugged his daughter and said goodbye to her and Thad. When the two men walked off, Leo Jensen didn't look back.

If Amanda was aware of the ramrod's anger, she gave no indication of it. She smiled at Thad as she took his hand and the two began to stroll toward the restaurant. The stroll would not be short. The church was located about a half mile north of Tin Cup's main street. 'I'm glad Sheriff Clausen gave you the whole day off.'

Thad returned the smile. 'Yes. It was very kind of him and Rance. They are working by themselves today.'

Amanda's smile diminished, replaced by curiosity. 'Are you men any closer to finding the killer of Mr Jensen and Mr Sherman?'

'Rance does have an interesting theory,' Thad answered. 'You see, a few hours after Sherman was killed, the cook at Art Sherman's ranch was up early to fix breakfast for the crew. He spotted Sherman's horse standing, saddle and all, by the barn. He roused one of Art's sons, Dencel, who knew all about the Jimmy Ellis legend.'

Amanda held Thad's hand a bit tighter. 'Everybody knows the legend now. I'm surprised no one has written a song about it.'

Thad laughed and casually kicked a stone; they were still a fair distance from the boardwalk. 'Dencel rode directly to the cottonwood near the line shack and found his father's body. He had been shot four times. A sawbuck lay on his chest. The son returned and told his mother and brother, Joshua, what had happened and then left for town to get Sheriff Clausen.'

'I know this sounds crazy, but in a way, Patty Sherman is a lucky woman,' Amanda said. 'She has always handled the books for the ranch and her two sons are now capable of running things without their father.'

The couple stepped on to the boardwalk and Thad resumed his story. 'Sheriff Clausen, Rance and me got out there as quick as we could. That's when Rance came up with his theory.'

Amanda gave her companion a look of rapt attention. For a moment, Thad thought about taking a little bit of credit for the theory himself, but quickly discarded the notion. 'Rance looked over the area carefully. He thinks Art Sherman's body was not dumped under the cottonwood. The way Dehner sees it, Sherman rode out to the cottonwood and was shot down right there. Something similar might have happened to Jed Coogan.'

They reached the Beecher Hotel and Thad held the door open for Amanda, who did not look impressed by what he had just told her. 'But why would Mr Coogan and Mr Sherman ride out there? That shack is only used a few months out of the year by the Rocking S.'

Thad stepped behind his companion and they walked towards the restaurant. 'Rance's notion does sort of break down.' Thad was grateful that he hadn't accepted any credit for the theory himself. Humility does have its rewards, he mused.

Following the evening service at the First Church of Tin Cup, Reverend Levi Davis remained outside the small building talking with various members of his congregation. Many of them really didn't want to go home. Levi was too intelligent to believe their hesitation in departing had anything to do with him or, for that matter, with the religious zeal of the church's membership. Many folks around Tin Cup lived on small, ten cow ranches that were scattered about. It could be a lonely existence and Sunday was often their only day to come together and socialize.

After everyone had left, Reverend Davis returned to the church and headed for his office to retrieve a broom. He would have to clean up now for Monday's meeting of the Temperance Union. Levi Davis was also Tin Cup's schoolmaster. Tomorrow, he'd be teaching until late afternoon, then ride out to the Sherman Ranch to visit Patty and the two boys, and then return to Tin Cup to preside at the meeting.

The pastor ran his broom between the first and second pews. His thoughts were on the church gossips who, on that day, had received some real meat to chew. Thad Brookshire had accompanied Amanda Shaw to both the morning and evening services. If only people would pay more attention to scripture, instead of. . . .

Levi Davis stopped sweeping. The broom handle pointed at him like an accusing finger. He needed to be honest with himself. He was jealous of Thad Brookshire. Levi had to work at not allowing his eyes to remain on Amanda Shaw while he preached, and not paying undue attention to her during the social time that followed the services was even tougher.

Reverend Davis unconsciously placed a hand on his receding hairline and sighed deeply. The foolish notions a beautiful woman can give a man! Why would Amanda Shaw have any interest in him? At thirty-three he was probably too old for her, and he looked older every time he used a comb and a patch of hair came out.

Levi clenched his teeth and said a brief prayer, asking for the will power to focus on his duties. He sang hymns to an empty sanctuary while he cleaned it. He then turned out the kerosene lamps that were fastened along the walls and retreated to his office.

Placing the broom in a corner, his eyes drifted to the cot where he slept every night. He gave a caustic laugh. 'I don't think Amanda would be very interested in sharing my life,' the pastor said to the rumpled blankets.

For that matter, what woman would, he wondered.

But Reverend Davis's prayer was being answered. His thoughts quickly shifted to the work he had to do before flopping on to the cot. The moonbeam that squeezed through a small window in the office did not provide enough light. He lit the lantern that hung on a nail over his desk and sat down to look over his notes for tomorrow's class.

The pastor would be teaching on the Magna Carta: a very important lesson. He began to meticulously review his notes.

Levi opened his eyes and his hands shot up as if he were being robbed. He didn't know how long he had been sleeping, but the flame on the lantern wasn't low. He couldn't have been asleep long.

Footsteps sounded from the sanctuary. The pastor bolted from his chair. Someone was coming to get him because of an emergency.

No. The footsteps weren't approaching the office. They were swift, and moving about the church. He could hear occasional bangs. Someone seemed to be intentionally piling things on to the floor.

The pastor felt afraid, but knew he had to remain calm. He mentally prayed for wisdom and protection as he removed an old Remington six shooter from a drawer in his desk. He took the lantern off the nail.

Stepping out of his office, Levi could hear a brief scrambling of feet. Apparently, the intruder had not known that the Pastor of First Church also lived there. He knew now.

Davis moved into the sanctuary and stood in front of the pulpit. Only a few hours ago, the pastor had stood in that pulpit and preached on loving your enemy. He wondered if that instruction might apply here.

The pastor held up the lantern and surveyed the small sanctuary. There were five pews on each side of a centre aisle. Heaped in the middle of that aisle was a collection of hymnals. Why would anyone toss hymnals into a pile like that? Terror suddenly scorched through Levi Davis. The intruder had planned to start a fire!

Levi tightened his grip on the gun as he shouted, 'Whoever you are, I know you're here. You're crouched down somewhere between the pews. Now stand up with your hands high. I don't want to use this gun!'

Davis cringed. His voice had sounded squeaky, revealing his fear. He tried again, consciously keeping his voice lower. 'I mean it!'

He still sounded scared and confused. The pastor gave up on having the intruder surrender. Holding the lantern high and his gun at waist level, Davis began to walk down the center aisle examining the areas between the pews.

The pastor remained alert for any movement. Davis figured the intruder would probably make a run for the door. Levi wondered if he could actually fire the gun. He hated hunting animals, how could he ever shoot at a man?

Davis tripped over some of the hymnals; as he grabbed a pew for support he heard a pinging sound. Levi turned and saw a small object wobble and then lie still on the floor near the last pew on his left side. He hurried toward the object which was now lying between the last pew and the one in front of it.

Davis placed the lantern on the pew. The kerosene light reflected off the silver coin as the pastor crouched down and picked it up. The pastor's voice was now a whisper. 'A half dollar! That ridiculous legend of Jimmy Ellis—'

An explosion ignited in Reverend Davis's head. He slammed face first into the floor and felt a boot press hard against his back. His Remington landed on the floor far away.

'Legend's got it right, sky pilot. This here's Jimmy Ellis. I pushed my way out of the grave. Got a few things to do before I go back there.'

'I don't believe you.'

'You don't hafta believe me! Just call off the meeting for tomorra night.'

'Why?'

'No questions, do what I say!'

Levi felt the boot lift off of his back and heard retreating footsteps. The pastor then shocked himself. He buoyed on to his feet and ran after the figure that was wearing a duster and a hat pulled low.

The intruder was halfway out the front door when Levi jumped him from behind. The church had no porch; both men plunged to the ground. The intruder rolled away from the pastor, on to his back. Levi lunged, reaching for the bandanna that covered half of his attacker's face, but a hard punch to Davis's left eye sent him sprawling backwards.

Levi fought to retain consciousness as he heard his attacker scramble to his feet. Through exploding red blotches, Davis saw the strange figure look down upon him.

'Stick to your Bible thumping, sky pilot, you ain't no fighter.' The speaker was now a shadow in the moonlight. 'And, remember, no meeting tomorra night or any night.'

The figure landed a hard kick to Davis's ribs then ran off. The pastor struggled to his feet and tried to follow his attacker. He meandered for a few yards and then collapsed.

Levi spoke to himself in a voice that was barely audible. 'I guess Jimmy's right. I'm no fighter.'

Proving himself wrong, he once again fought back on to his feet and began a long, hard walk to the sheriff's office.

CHAPTER THIRTEEN

Reverend Davis stood outside the church and greeted the large crowd arriving for the Temperance Union meeting. The pastor made jokes about his swollen eye. 'Whoever hit me was no spirit from the grave, but I am grateful to him. It looks like he boosted our attendance tonight, though I am quite sure that was not his intention.'

Rance Dehner smiled benignly as he listened from a few feet away to Davis's brave words. Dehner had little enthusiasm for the temperance movement, but he admired Levi Davis. Reverend Davis was the kind of man the west desperately needed: a man who brought a message of peace and devoted himself to educating children.

Of course, in order to achieve their goals, men like Levi Davis needed to stay alive. That was where his job came in.

The meeting was scheduled to start in a few minutes. As they had planned in advance, Dehner, Harry and Thad huddled together in front of the church. Harry Clausen spoke in a loud voice. That was hardly unusual. The sheriff's voice had a natural boom to it. But on this night, the loudness served a specific purpose.

'Once we get inside, I'll stand on the right side of the church, down towards the front. Thad, I want you to be standing on the left side near the middle. Dehner, you stand in the back. That way, we should be able to handle any trouble in case that fella that attacked the Reverend shows up tonight.'

Brookshire and Dehner both nodded in agreement. The crowd began to move into the church and seat themselves in the pews. Dehner entered last leaving the door ajar behind him.

Reverend Davis hurried to the front of the church. 'I know all of you have a busy day ahead tomorrow, so let's get started. We are here to discuss matters that are very important to our community. Matters on which there is strong disagreement. Let's open our meeting with prayer, asking the Lord to guide us through our conflicts.'

As Levi began his prayer and all heads were bowed, Dehner quietly slipped out of the church. This time he closed the door behind him completely and scanned the area. The detective couldn't see anyone and heard nothing unusual. But he knew he had to move quickly. The moon was bright and the church didn't have an overhang to cloak him in shade.

Dehner sprinted toward a large sycamore tree that stood several yards to the side of the church. He recalled what Harry Clausen had told him when they had concocted this scheme a few hours earlier. 'Climb to the top of that old sycamore and you'll get a great view of the whole area. And the tree ain't lost foliage yet, you can hide real good up there.'

As Rance lifted himself into the tree and began his ascent,

childhood memories flooded his thoughts. He smiled inwardly, recalling the mischief he and some buddies had wreaked from treetops.

The memories suddenly turned dark. His thoughts had skipped from childhood to the time when he was sixteen. He was serving as a deputy in a small, dusty town and mighty proud to be wearing a badge. One horrible day he got careless and a young woman, a woman he loved, died because of it. He would carry that day with him forever. . . .

Rance stopped and mentally chastized himself. He needed to keep his mind on his assignment. A dangerous killer was loose. If he allowed himself to wallow in the past, more innocents could get killed.

The detective climbed to the highest elevation the tree branches would allow and looked downward. Harry Clausen had been right. Dehner's perch afforded an excellent view. He could even look over the church and see any movement on the opposite side. He also had a good view of the long, narrow line of forest that ran along the back of the church.

Rance remained as still as he could. There was no wind that night and he didn't want rustling leaves to give away the scheme he had cooked up with Harry Clausen and Thad Brookshire. The three men figured the killer would be mingling with the crowd outside the church before the meeting. He would hear Harry give his deputies their instructions and feel free to strike from outside.

At least that was how the lawmen hoped the situation would play out. As he kept a careful eye on the scene below, Rance gave himself mental sermons on the importance of patience in detective work. He had never enjoyed spending a lot of time just watching a location.

Watching from a tree was even less enjoyable.

To Dehner it seemed like hours, but after a wait of about

ten minutes a figure leading a horse emerged from the forest. The detective tensed up. The figure was wearing a duster and a hat pulled low. Rance would be willing to bet that the bottom half of the stranger's face was covered by a bandanna.

And Dehner figured the newcomer wasn't really a stranger.

The newcomer untied something from his saddle and began to approach the back of the church. From Dehner's vantage point, the figure seemed to be carrying a small bale of hay. He was going to take a second try at starting a fire.

Rance started to climb down the tree, but a branch snapped beneath his foot. The potential arsonist looked towards the sycamore and reached for his gun, sending a shot into the branches. The figure had not been able to see Dehner. The detective clung to the tree trunk as a bullet zinged harmlessly through the leaves.

Cries and sounds of confusion blared from within the church. As Dehner climbed down the tree he could hear a shout resound over the ruckus. 'Stop acting like fools or Jimmy Ellis will return!'

As Rance hit the ground, he could see the man who called himself Jimmy Ellis drop the bale of hay and run for his horse. He had a head start on the detective, but Ellis was not a fast runner. Dehner took after him.

Rance had almost caught up with his prey when Ellis mounted his horse and spurred the roan into a gallop. Dehner took a few more fast steps, leapt at the steed and grabbed the rider by his arm. The roan stumbled, then continued trying to run.

Ellis dropped the horse's reins and tried to deliver a punch to his attacker. The punch went wild and destroyed the rider's precarious balance. Ellis plunged off the roan, taking Dehner with him.

As they hit the ground, both men scrambled to their feet. Ellis once again broke into a desperate run, this time back toward the forest. Dehner tackled him and laughed when his prey broke into a string of obscenities.

'I never realized ghosts used such language.' Dehner spoke as he buoyed back on to his feet, palmed his Colt and ripped the bandanna off the ghost's face.

CHAPTER FOURTEEN

Harry Clausen and Rance Dehner stepped from the jail area into the office portion of the sheriff's office. Three men were waiting for them: Thad Brookshire, Levi Davis and Peter Kyle. All of the men were standing. The pastor and the bar owner looked tense. Thad's face reflected no emotion at all.

The sheriff took note of his deputy's blank slate and felt proud. Thad was turning into a fine lawman.

Clausen quickly put such thoughts aside. There was important business to attend to. The sheriff headed for his desk and stood behind it. He drummed his fingers on the scarred desktop for a moment and faced the others. He wanted this meeting to be reasonably informal. He first addressed Peter Kyle.

'Your bartender, Otto, has confessed to assaultin' Reverend Davis and tryin' to set fire to the church tonight, but he claims that's it. We've established that Otto has alibis for the nights Jed Coogan and Art Sherman were killed. He was tendin' bar while there was all night poker games goin' on. Many of the men involved in those poker games were at the church tonight. Not hard to question them.'

Clausen inhaled deeply and gave quick glances to his deputies. Dehner stood beside the desk, his face as passive as that of Thad Brookshire. A mood of forced casualness filled the office.

The sheriff continued. 'Otto says he did what he did because he wanted to stop the temperance movement. He thought those people would get their way and he'd be out of a job.'

Kyle shook his head. 'Otto has had a tough life. When I made him a partner he figured he was getting a break at last. Then he saw it all falling apart, or thought he did. Since this Jimmy Ellis stuff has the whole town spooked, I guess Otto thought he could use it to stop the temperance people.'

Levi Davis slammed a fist into his left palm. 'This is all my fault!'

'What do you mean, Reverend?' Rance asked.

'I have been . . . well . . . deceptive. My deception may have harmed Otto. As you gentlemen know, I have been supportive of the temperance movement. I have witnessed many lives that were destroyed by alcohol, including that of my father. So, I support many of the goals of the temperance crowd.'

A look of understanding flashed in Dehner's eyes. 'You support many of their goals but not all of them.'

The pastor closed his eyes for a moment as if experiencing a painful spasm. He still looked in pain when those eyes reopened. 'In a way, Otto is right. The temperance people actually want to make liquor illegal. Can you imagine the horror such a situation would bring about?'

Thad pushed his hat a few inches back on his head. 'I don't follow you.'

Levi pointed an index finger in the air as if making a point in a sermon. 'If liquor was banned, people could make a fortune selling rotgut: booze produced in stills made from who knows what. Rotgut kills enough people already.'

Dehner's eyes shifted between Peter Kyle and Levi Davis. 'I suspect you two gentlemen had a little agreement.'

Peter Kyle nodded and looked amused. Levi Davis nodded, but looked embarrassed. 'Like I confessed earlier, I practiced deception,' the pastor said. 'I don't want liquor banned, but I want it controlled.'

Kyle seemed concerned by Davis's unease. 'After I bought the Paradise, I had a little talk with the Reverend. We agreed that I would soon meet with the temperance union. I'd promise not to open my saloons on Sunday. I would stay open into the wee hours of Sunday morning, but once I closed, I wouldn't open again until Monday.'

'I want Sunday to be a family day,' Levi explained. 'A lot of people come in from the ranches on Sunday and attend both the morning and evening services. They eat lunch at the café or hotel restaurant. After that, many of the men gather in a saloon and leave their wives and kids on their own. The men spend enough time in saloons already!'

Dehner smiled sympathetically. 'That plan would also help to calm down the hotheads in the temperance movement.'

'Yes, that too,' the pastor said.

Peter Kyle spoke in an almost mischievous manner. 'I'll let you gents in on a little secret. I'm sure a lot of saloon owners in the east secretly like the blue laws: laws that order them to close on Sunday. Truth is, the profits on Sunday are pretty low. Men just jaw on Sunday, they don't drink or gamble all that much. Besides, the people who own saloons and the people who work in them need time off, too.'

'Was Otto aware of this here scheme of yours?' the sheriff asked.

Both the pastor and the bar owner shook their heads.

Clausen patted his desk a few times as if it were a friendly dog and then continued to speak. 'I believe Otto when he said he didn't know Reverend Davis slept in his office at the church. Tonight, he planned to start a fire behind the church. He was sure everyone would get out before the flames spread. In both cases he planned to wait until people were trying to put out the blaze, then he would gallop by dressed as the ghost of Jimmy Ellis and shout out a warning about the Temperance Union. That's very dangerous shenanigans.'

'Small children and fools shouldn't play with fire,' Thad said.

Harry Clausen smiled and looked at his deputy in agreement. 'Exactly. I'm holdin' Otto in jail 'til the circuit judge gets here next week.' He turned his eyes to the saloon owner. 'Pete, I'm 'fraid your bartender is gonna be spendin' a few years in jail. He claims he panicked when he shot at Dehner and didn't intend to kill him. Still. . . .'

Levi Davis sighed deeply. 'I wonder, if all this horrible craziness hadn't happened, would Otto have gone loco the way he did? The man was deeply troubled but—'

Dehner gently cut in. 'When there is a string of sensational crimes like this town is seeing right now, it does set some people off. They try to duplicate the acts.'

'Meanwhile, the fella who's playing ghost is still out there,' Harry Clausen said.

The five men continued to talk for about fifteen minutes, repeating facts and opinions. As the meeting gradually broke up, Dehner noted that Levi Davis still appeared remorseful over what he termed deception. Rance figured the pastor wouldn't be getting much sleep that night.

After the reverend and the bar owner were gone, Clausen spoke to his deputies. 'Why don't the two of you do a round together? This has been a pretty crazy night, who knows what fool notions are in some jasper's head?'

As Dehner and Brookshire stepped out of the sheriff's office and made their way up the boardwalk, the detective observed the confident demeanor of his companion. Thad was feeling increasingly comfortable in his position as a western lawman. Rance wondered how much longer he should wait before telling Thad about his father.

Dehner's private musings were quickly shattered. Thad suddenly stopped, his eyes fixed on a newcomer who was riding into town.

'Oh, no!' Thad's voice was a faint whisper.

'What's wrong?'

For a moment, Thad didn't answer Dehner's question. He stood in frozen silence, staring straight ahead.

CHAPTER FIFTEEN

Thad Brookshire and Amanda Shaw rode together in a comfortable silence. They were headed for an isolated location where they had been a few times before. This was becoming a familiar ride for the horses and the animals moved briskly, not requiring much direction. Amanda broke the silence with a giggle.

'What are you laughing about?' Thad asked in feigned anger.

'Do you read much poetry?'

Thad's turn to laugh. 'Use to. I didn't have much choice in the matter. A teacher of mine was crazy about John Donne. "No man is an island." I guess Mr Donne had a point.' He looked directly at Amanda. 'I sure don't want to be an island.'

Amanda smiled back and another silence, this one intense, was shared by the couple. The young woman slowly looked away and returned to her reflections. 'I've read John Donne too, but I prefer the romantic poets: the ones who write about holding hands in the moonlight and making a wish together on a star. We haven't had much of a chance to do any of that.'

Thad glanced at the dawn light filling the sky. 'Well, you have to spend most days here at your ranch and I have my duties in town. A picnic breakfast is about the only chance we have to see each other. As far as I'm concerned, it's the best time of the day.'

Amanda didn't hesitate with her reply. 'I agree.'

The couple continued to ride as the flat land took a slight dip. They were now in sight of four scraggy trees that were bunched together a few yards back from a stream. The smell of water prodded the horses to move faster. When Amanda spoke again her voice was filled with concern. 'You've been sort of quiet this morning. Is anything bothering you? From what you told me things turned out OK at the temperance meeting, despite all that trouble.'

'It's not that.'

'Then what is it?'

Thad gritted his teeth, and when he spoke again his voice

was angry. 'That fool writer Foster Lewis is back in Tin Cup. I spotted him riding into town last night while Rance and I were doing a round.'

'Did you talk to him?'

'Yes. Rance wasn't any happier to see him than I was. We both questioned the man. He acted innocent as a pup, said he was doing research for some article. Lewis hasn't broken any law, so there's nothing we can do. . . .'

'Does Foster Lewis look like that drawing of him in the magazine?'

'Yes, pretty much.' Thad's head suddenly jerked in the direction of his companion. 'Do you have a copy of *Real Gunfighters!*? The one about the Lightning Kid?'

'Well . . . yes.'

'Why?'

Amanda looked away from Thad and gently patted her horse. 'I enjoy reading it and rereading it.'

'But it's all a pack of lies!'

'Not all of it.'

'Most of it!'

The young woman continued to look at the back of her horse's head. 'I'm going to keep the magazine. I think some day it would be fun to show it to . . . some people.'

'Who?'

The couple arrived at their destination and the question went unanswered. Amada dismounted and removed a picnic basket she had tied to her saddle. 'You take care of the horses,' she said playfully to Thad. 'I'll get the grub ready.' Amanda laughed as she ran under the shade provided by the trees.

About fifteen minutes later, the horses had enjoyed a drink at the stream and their reins were tethered under a pile of stones. Thad and Amanda were sitting on a thin blanket enjoying a breakfast of biscuits and ham accompanied by cherry pie.

'These biscuits are sure something special,' Thad said. 'Just about everyone in town talks about how well you can bake.'

'Oh,' Amanda replied coyly. 'Have you been asking questions about my cooking?'

'Maybe.'

'And just why was that?'

The horses neighed and Brookshire thought he heard approaching footsteps. He jumped to his feet and drew his gun. The footsteps stopped. Whoever it was knew that his presence was no longer a secret.

The footsteps continued at a slower more cautious pace until a figure stepped into view. 'Well, good morning Mr Jensen, out for a morning stroll?' Thad spoke as he holstered his gun.

Leo Jensen eyed Thad with total hatred. It occurred to the deputy that hate seemed to be the only way Jensen ever regarded him. 'I'm here to take Miss Shaw back to the ranch where her father wants her to be.'

Amanda gracefully rose to her feet. 'What are you talking about?'

The ramrod pointed a finger at Amanda. 'Don't you remember the night Mr Shaw went to the meeting in the sheriff's office? Your father tole you not to keep company with no lawman!'

A smirk of recall jumped across Amanda's face. 'Mr Jensen, you're making something out of nothing.'

'No I ain't!' Jensen dropped his hand to his side, near his gun.

Amanda seemed to realize that her statement could have sounded harsh. She lowered her voice. 'When you and

Father returned from the meeting, I fixed you both some pie and coffee. While I was pouring the Java, Father said the idea of my seeing a lawman made him nervous. It was an offhand remark.'

'Didn't sound offhand to me.'

Amanda gave the ramrod a kind smile. 'Mr Jensen, I appreciate all that you do. Father told me about how you stayed up with him most of that night listening to his army stories. Stories I'm sure you've heard a hundred times before. You are very valuable to the Rocking S, but you're not my big brother. Please keep that in mind.'

'What I got in mind is that you're coming back with me. Now!'

The kind approach had not worked. Thad decided to handle the matter differently. 'Where's your horse, Jensen?'

Leo pointed away from the stream. 'Yonder.'

'You could see the horses belonging to Miss Shaw and myself tethered nearby. So, you dismounted and tried to sneak up on us. I think you have a real wicked mind, Leo.'

'Whaddya mean?'

'You thought you'd catch Miss Shaw and me spooning under these trees, or maybe something even more than that. Then you could run back and report to your boss. He'd be outraged. Miss Shaw would be shamed. Any future Miss Shaw and I might have had together would be out the window and you'd be a happy man.'

'You're loco.'

'I'm sounding a lot more sane than you are. Light a shuck, Jensen.'

'Is that there an order . . . Deputy?'

Thad took off his badge and placed it in his shirt pocket. 'I'm speaking as a friend of Miss Shaw.'

'You're still wearing a hogleg.'

'I'll take off my gunbelt if you do the same, then we can settle this in a civilized manner, with fists.'

Both men unbuckled their gunbelts and dropped them to the ground. As Amanda shouted 'No' several times, both men held up their fists and began to circle one another.

Jensen took the first swing: hard, fast and too wide. The ramrod had put a lot of weight into it and he was thrown off balance. Thad replied with a quick jab which his opponent only partially ducked. Most of Thad's fist collided with Leo's jaw and the ramrod spun and belly flopped on to the ground.

'Stop it, both of you!' Amanda ran in front of Thad and placed a hand on his chest. She then looked down at Leo Jensen. 'Mr Jensen, I have never given you an order before, but I am now. Get back to the ranch. If you leave now, I will tell Father nothing about this.'

Jensen began to rise to his feet. 'This jasper got lucky—'

'I said, leave now!'

Leo picked up his gunbelt and looked at Thad. 'This ain't finished.' He stomped off.

Thad and Amanda stepped to where they could see Leo mount his horse and ride off. Not until the ramrod was completely out of sight did Amanda turn to her companion, 'Are you OK?'

'Sure. Leo was right about one thing. I did get lucky.'

'Well, Mr Lucky, you still need some breakfast.'

The couple settled back down on the blanket. The mood was now more sombre. After Thad finished eating a biscuit he looked nervously at Amanda. 'Something I said to Jensen makes me feel . . . well . . . makes me feel kind of rotten inside.'

'What's that?'

'I accused Leo of trying to catch us kissing and all.'

Amanda shrugged her shoulders. 'I'm sure you were right.'

Thad looked at the branches that hung over them. 'Yes, but, I have to admit, in my mind I've been thinking about that, been thinking about it a lot.'

The deputy looked around for a few moments before he had to courage to once again look Amanda in the eye. When he did, he found the young woman smiling at him.

'I have too,' she said.

CHAPTER SIXTEEN

My Dearest Mitzi

I have, at last, come upon a very fortuitous circumstance which I am sure will allow us to be married and live very comfortably for the rest of our days.

As you will recall, I came to the town of Tin Cup to do a story about a poor boy bringing down the Lightning Kid, the son of a rich man and an exploiter of the poor, in a dramatic gun duel. To my tremendous surprise, I have discovered an even better story already unfolding in this wretched town.

The local denizens believe that the ghost of a man hung here twenty years ago has returned from the dead to inflict revenge on the men who strung him up. I am not exactly sure how these yokels fell into such superstitious notions, but I plan to investigate this story and make it mine exclusively.

As you well know the life of a writer can be one of frustration and disappointment. People often do not understand or appreciate the difficult art of writing. But I know I can present this story in such a way that it will win me great success and allow you to resign from the Crystal Palace. We will be able to have the life together that we have always wanted.

Love Always, Foster.

Foster Lewis took great care in signing his first name to the letter. He wanted it to have a dramatic flow and yet look distinguished.

He addressed an envelope, placed the letter inside and then left his second floor hotel room, letter in hand. When he had checked in, Lewis had been informed that the hotel took care of letters for its guests.

As he plodded down the hall toward the stairway, Foster began to worry. Mitzi would not tolerate another failure. This time, he had to succeed.

The writer realized he had no idea as to the next step for pursuing the story about the ghost of Jimmy Ellis. He had already spent most of a night talking to barflies at the Gold Coin. There probably wasn't much more to be mined there. What next?

He could try interviewing the sheriff, but that was an iffy prospect. Foster had already jawed with Tin Cup's two deputies and that hadn't gone well. They seemed inclined to run him out of town.

Clomping down the stairs, Foster ruminated over an uncomfortable truth. The better the lawman, the less inclined he was to jaw with a writer. The blowhards were the ones who gave him the best stories. And, from his brief encounter with Harry Clausen during his last trip to Tin Cup, Foster Lewis had learned that Clausen was no blowhard.

But Thad Brookshire was now a deputy! If this ghost thing fell through, that could aid his original scheme. At the first chance, he would pay a visit to Boone Estey. The moonshiner would be easy enough to find, and he might still need him to play the poor, but virtuous hero.

As he reached the ground floor, Lewis could hear the desk clerk proclaim, 'Why, there he is now!' Foster smiled gallantly at the young lady waiting for him in the lobby. A woman this beautiful could only be bringing good luck.

Harry Clausen shook with laughter as he listened to Thad's account of his picnic breakfast that morning. 'So, despite all his tough talk, Leo Jensen flopped down like a sack of potatoes when you hit him.'

'He sure did,' Brookshire replied. 'Surprised me.'

'I think you're the one who surprised Leo,' the sheriff spoke as he continued to laugh.

Harry was sitting behind his desk. Thad walked around the office as he told his story. Dehner was perched on the desk's front edge. The detective had not enjoyed Thad's narrative as much as the sheriff, though he couldn't put a finger on the reason why.

'Do you and Miss Shaw breakfast together often?' Rance asked.

'Whenever we can. Of course, on mornings when I have to do the early round. . . .'

'Why didn't you say so!' Clausen boomed. 'Between us, Rance and I can handle the early round.' He looked at the detective. 'You don't mind rousing the drunks that have slept it off behind the Gold Coin do you?'

Dehner smirked and shrugged his shoulders. 'Can't think

of a more pleasant way to greet the day.'

'Thanks, gents,' Thad said. 'You're both being very kind.'

'Yes, you are both very kind men.' Amanda Shaw smiled brightly as she entered the office.

Thad was stunned to see the woman. 'What're you doing here?'

The smile turned playful. 'Aren't you happy to see me?'

'Yes, of course, but when I left you at the Rocking S—'

'When you left me, I went right inside the house and had a long talk with Father.'

'But you said you weren't going to tell Mr Shaw anything about what Leo Jensen tried—'

Amanda waved a hand as if dismissing an insignificant fact. 'I didn't talk to him about Leo. Didn't have to. You put Leo Jensen in his place.'

Both Harry Clausen and Rance Dehner were now on their feet. Harry spoke in a good natured voice. 'Thad, I think this young lady has somethin' to say. Why don't you stop askin' questions for a moment or so and give her a chance to tell us what's on her mind?' The sheriff motioned to a chair in front of his desk. 'Would you care to sit down Miss Shaw?'

'No thank you, Sheriff Clausen. I'm too excited to sit down.'

Clausen tilted his head in a questioning manner. 'What's got you so all riled up?'

Amanda clasped her hands together in a prayer like gesture 'After talking with Father this morning, I came into town and saw Mr Foster Lewis.'

'What?' Thad looked flabbergasted. 'You spent time with that liar?'

The young woman's body went stiff and she placed her clasped hands against her breast as if bracing for an assault.

'He isn't a liar. Not exactly.'

Thad wasn't appeased. 'What do you mean, "not exactly?" '

Amanda inhaled and then spoke in a somewhat prim matter. 'Mr Lewis explained to me that he sometimes adds fictional accounts to his stories for the sake of dramatic emphasis.'

'Oh brother!' Thad threw those words at the ceiling.

Dehner spoke in a soft voice, trying to calm the atmosphere. 'Miss Shaw, why did you go to see Mr Lewis?'

Amanda unclasped her hands and dropped them to her sides. She appeared grateful for Rance's gentle demeanour. 'Like I said, after breakfast I had a long talk with Father. He wants to . . . well . . . tell the world, so to speak, about what happened twenty years ago to Jimmy Ellis.'

Dehner's voice remained soft. 'Your father believes telling his story to Foster Lewis would, in a way, clear the air.'

'Exactly,' the young woman responded. 'But he doesn't feel right doing it unless the other men involved agree to talk with Mr Lewis too. That's why I came into town.'

Harry Clausen nervously ran a hand through his hair. 'You're gonna talk with Clarence Newton, Peter Kyle and Beau Haney about spillin' it all to this writer?'

The woman's reply sounded confident and even cheerful. 'I sure am! I'm going to talk with Reverend Davis about it, too.'

'What does the pastor have to do with Jimmy Ellis?' Rance asked.

Amanda went quiet for a moment. She seemed to be struggling with how to explain the clergyman's involvement. 'Father wants all of this to happen in the church with a preacher right there. He regards it as a confession of sin before both God and man.'

Dehner's face turned sombre. 'I'm sure God will forgive what happened twenty years ago, but I'm not so sure about the law. There is no statute of limitations when it comes to murder. A confession could cost those men their freedom, maybe even their lives.'

Amanda Shaw did not look worried. 'The hanging took place twenty years ago,' she said. 'Everyone agrees that Jimmy Ellis brutally murdered men, women and children. Two of the men who will be confessing have made up for what they did by becoming outstanding citizens. Beau Haney has become a drunk, inflicting punishment on himself. I don't think the law will take any action.'

'She's got a point there, Rance,' the sheriff hastily added. 'I'm sure the law will do nothin'.'

Dehner nodded his head. 'When do you plan to have this meeting, Miss Shaw?'

'I'm hoping for late tomorrow afternoon, after Reverend Davis has finished teaching.'

'There's something else to keep in mind,' Dehner said. 'If this meeting comes off, all of the men involved in hanging Jimmy Ellis will be together in one room. Potential targets for the killer who's posing as Ellis.'

The confidence which had resided in Amanda's face diminished a bit. 'Yes, you're right, that's one reason I'm here now.'

The woman's statement was met with silence. She continued, 'I was wondering, Sheriff Clausen, if you could promise that you or one of your deputies would attend the meeting. That way, everyone would be as safe as they were when they attended that get together here in your office.'

'Sure,' the sheriff said. 'I can make that promise.'

Amanda gave a quick glance towards Thad Brookshire. The young woman seemed unable to read whatever signs were on Thad's face and returned her eyes to Harry Clausen. 'I was also wondering Sheriff if . . . maybe . . . you'd ask one of your deputies to accompany me on my talks with the gentlemen in question. I believe the presence of a deputy would be reassuring.'

Amusement brightened Sheriff Clausen's countenance, but he managed to sound completely serious when he spoke: 'Thad, would you please accompany Miss Shaw?'

Thad Brookshire fidgeted nervously. A plethora of emotions shot through him. He felt ridiculous and embarrassed over the way he had blown up at the girl. Still, he wished she had talked with him before launching this crazy plan.

He wanted to get back in her good graces, to get back to where they had been only a few hours ago. For the first time since he had yelled at her, Thad looked directly into Amanda's eyes and spoke. 'I'd be happy to.'

The couple smiled at each other awkwardly and left the office without speaking. The moment they had departed, Clausen broke out in laughter. 'I'll bet Thad is fumblin' his way through an apology right now.'

Dehner ran a hand over the back of his neck. 'This idea Miss Shaw has come up with, it could be dangerous.'

'That Amanda Shaw is not only a looker, she's smart too!' The sheriff continued speaking. He hadn't heard a word Dehner had just said. 'She knows Thad Brookshire is head and shoulders above most of the men in this town.'

Dehner agreed, then left the office to do a round. His mind was very much on Sheriff Harry Clausen. The lawman had certainly been very solicitous towards Amanda Shaw. Nothing wrong with that, but. . . .

Rance silently cursed himself for being so dense. Of course! Clausen wanted Thad to marry Amanda. That development would practically guarantee Thad spending the rest of his life in Tin Cup, or at least the sheriff probably looked at it that way.

Harry Clausen was a great sheriff and a lonely man. He probably looked upon Thad as the son he'd never had.

Dehner stopped at the Tin Cup Community Bank and went inside. Everything seemed to be in order. Rance strolled around, smiled and exchanged pleasantries with the customers and staff. This was a normal part of his rounds.

Outside the bank, Dehner stopped smiling and didn't feel at all pleasant. The detective felt he was betraying both Thad Brookshire and Harry Clausen. He had originally planned to wait until the Jimmy Ellis matter was settled before telling Thad Brookshire his real reason for being in Tin Cup: William Brookshire's doctors had told him he had about one year to live. The businessman wanted to see his son before he died.

The detective felt he had handled the matter poorly. If Thad wanted to delay seeing his father until the killer posing as Jimmy Ellis was caught, that was fine, but the decision should be Thad's.

Dehner sighed and pulled on his ear. He wasn't looking forward to it, but later in the day he needed to have a serious talk with Thad Brookshire.

Thad tied up his horse to the fence that ran in front of the Rocking S ranch house. He quickly wiped his eyes with both hands. He had cried some on his ride out to the ranch and didn't want any trace of tears to be visible.

He opened the gate and walked to the front door. This visit was unplanned. The deputy wondered what Abner Shaw would think of him calling well after sundown. For that matter, he wondered what Amanda would think. His behavior was certainly improper.

But he had to see the woman.

Thad saw Amanda's beautiful face fill the living room window of the ranch house. She opened the front door and was waiting for him as he stepped on to the porch.

'Thad, what's wrong?'

Brookshire gave no thought to how she knew something was wrong. 'Amanda, I'm sorry but I need to talk with you . . . alone.'

'Well . . . yes . . . of course . . . just give me a minute.'

She closed the door and from inside, Thad could hear her voice.

'Thad's outside, he wants to talk. I won't be long, Father.'

The deputy could hear Abner's frail voice, but not what he was saying.

Amanda's reply sounded kind and firm. 'I don't know, but I'm sure it's important.'

The young woman reappeared on the porch and took Thad's hand. 'It's a lovely night out. Let's take a walk.'

As they stepped off the porch, Thad immediately began to apologize. 'I can understand if you are angry about me coming out here so late—'

'I'm not angry at all. After all, this was an important day for us.'

'What do you mean?'

'Why, this morning we had our first argument. In the sheriff's office, off all places!'

Thad smiled as he opened the gate, allowed Amanda to go through first, and then closed it behind them. 'I guess we did at that.'

The couple once again joined hands. At Thad's leading they walked towards the corral, which was on the opposite side of the ranch from the bunkhouse. The young man wanted their conversation to be private, but he wasn't quite ready to get to the point yet. 'Despite my stupid behaviour this morning, we did get a lot done.'

'Yes,' Amanda said. 'All of the men involved in hanging Jimmy Ellis agreed to talk with Foster Lewis tomorrow and Reverend Davis will be there. My father believes this will be an important step in ending the matter, as much as it can be ended.'

'If we're really going to end the legend of Jimmy Ellis, we've got to stop whoever it is that's killing in his name.'

Amanda nodded her head. She knew Thad was leading up to something else, something important, but she didn't know what.

The couple arrived at the corral. There were two horses inside, both of which hurried to Amanda. The young woman laughed as she patted the nags. 'Sorry, no apple tonight.'

The woman was still patting the horses when Thad began to speak. He told her the story of how he had run off from home and how Rance Dehner was a detective employed by William Brookshire. And he told Amanda the reason his father had hired Dehner.

When Amanda replied her voice was little more than a whisper. 'That's terrible, Thad. Your father only has a year left . . . I'm so sorry . . . what are you going to do?'

Thad made a fist and tapped it against the corral. 'I don't know. I feel so torn apart.'

'I don't understand.'

'I just can't abandon Sheriff Clausen until this Ellis thing is settled, but. . . .'

'Is Mr Dehner going to stay on to help Mr Clausen?' Amanda asked.

'Don't know. I got so upset by what he told me, I didn't ask. Of course, I told Sheriff Clausen about . . . everything . . . he looked troubled, but seemed happy when I promised to stay on for a while. . . .'

'Why did you leave home, Thad?'

'I've been doing some serious thinking about that lately, and don't care much for my conclusion. I think I ran off because I was afraid.'

'Afraid of what?'

Thad looked at the horses in the corral as he answered the question. 'My father was a war hero. He came home with one leg gone and another useless. . . .'

'Oh no. That must have been awful.'

'William Brookshire didn't let the loss of two legs stop him,' Thad continued. 'He went into business and became one of the wealthiest men in Texas. I was worried I couldn't measure up to what he had done. That's the real reason I took off.'

'You're right to wait until the killer who's posing as Jimmy Ellis gets caught, but Thad, you've got to go back and visit your father.'

'I know.'

Amanda looked at the ground for a moment, then looked back at Thad Brookshire as she took a couple of steps towards him. The two were now only inches apart. 'Thad, if it would help any . . . well . . . I'd be happy, I'd be proud to travel back to Dallas with you. I'd like to meet your father.'

Thad looked at the woman with something close to amazement. The two young people embraced and Thad Brookshire was no longer afraid of anything.

CHAPTER SEVENTEEN

Beau Haney cursed the night as he approached his house, but he spewed forth the profanity without passion. In truth, he was feeling good about himself. He had imbibed moderately that night, or moderately by his standards. He would be able to get up at sunrise and head out for Abbot's Livery. Stanley had told him he would need a lot of help in the morning.

'I won't letya down, Stanley,' Beau mumbled as he entered his house.

He eyed the couch in his living room with a smug sense of self-righteousness. On most nights he dropped on to that stuffed couch the moment he arrived home. Not tonight. He was still sober enough to take his clothes off and get into bed proper like.

Beau heard a slithering sound as if there was a large snake nearby. The entire room was suddenly in total darkness. Someone had closed the curtains on the house's front window.

A hard kick smashed against Beau's right ankle. He went down on his back and a heavy boot pressed against his chest. Beau could only see the outline of a dark figure standing over him, but he knew immediately who it was.

'Jimmy Ellis!' Beau's voice came out a terrified screech.

'That's right, Beau,' The figure replied with caustic amusement. 'You may be an old souse, but you're smarter than most folks in this two bit town.'

Beau's entire body was trembling. 'Whaddya mean?'

'Imagine, some people mistaking that fool bartender for me. What do I care if people drink or they don't drink? They can drink themselves to death for all I care. That's sort of the future you got in mind for yourself, right Beau?'

'Yes, Jimmy, that's right.'

The dark figure laughed, but there was no joy in it. 'I have a little plan to help you fulfill your life's ambition, Beau Haney. Yes, instead of me killing you, you'll live long enough to die lying on the floor with a bottle in your hand. The way a worthless souse should die.'

Haney began to weep. 'Please. . . .'

The boot pressed down harder on Beau's chest. The figure's voice became lower and harsher. 'Stop your damn blubbering and listen! Listen to me real careful. You're going to follow orders like a good deputy. Remember what you did to your deputy twenty years ago when he only tried to do his duty?'

Beau Haney said nothing, though he continued to weep. The boot left Haney's chest and kicked him in the left thigh.

'I asked you a question, Beau!'

The former lawman yelped in pain, crouched into a foetal position and moaned, 'Yes, I slugged Harry Clausen. . . .'

'I'll do a lot worse than slug you, Beau, a lot worse. Now, are you going to follow my orders?'

'Yes.'

The figure gave another joyless laugh. 'That's good, Beau, that's real good.'

Beau Haney's body continued to tremble.

CHAPTER EIGHTEEN

Foster Lewis stood beside the front door of the church basking in the attention he was receiving. He was surrounded by important people, all of them treating him with respect. Foster wished Mitzi could be here to witness all of this. She'd realize what an important man he was becoming.

The writer shook hands with Clarence Newton, the town banker, Peter Kyle, a highly successful businessman and Abner Shaw, the owner of a large ranch. The introductions weren't altogether delightful. Sheriff Harry Clausen and his deputy, the former Lightning Kid, were also present. Foster had already met them.

The proceedings were being directed by Reverend Davis and Amanda Shaw, who Foster knew was the driving force behind this meeting. He would have to send her a signed copy of the issue of *Real Gunfighters* that would carry the article. Perhaps he would even send her an edition of his book. He was certain that what he was to learn during his current stay in Tin Cup could be expanded into a book.

Levi Davis beamed an artificial cheerfulness as he made the introductions. The pastor had some doubts as to the wisdom of this meeting. But Deputy Brookshire had assured him it was a good idea and he wanted to help the town's lawmen as much as possible.

Of course, Amanda Shaw's magnificent smile had something to do with it too.

The pastor addressed Amanda when all the hand shaking

was done. 'Is Beau Haney joining us this afternoon?'

Amanda looked embarrassed, 'I dropped by Mr Haney's house about thirty minutes ago. He's . . . not feeling well.'

The woman's comments led to a few smirks which Reverend Davis ignored as he spoke to Foster Lewis. 'Mr Lewis, will you be able to conduct your interviews without the presence of Mr Haney?'

'I'm sure I can, Reverend. A writer must always be flexible and alert to any new challenge.' Haney's absence didn't bother Foster Lewis. He had spent enough of his life talking with barflies. Today, he would be interviewing people who really counted.

'Very well then,' the pastor continued in his forced jolliness, 'Let's get inside and get down to what we all came here for.' He opened the church door and motioned Amanda to enter first.

The seven men who ambled in behind the young woman all appeared a bit awkward. Levi tried to move things along. 'Miss Shaw thought sitting in pews would make it hard for us to see each other while we talk. It was her excellent suggestion to set up chairs on the platform.'

The pastor pointed to an arc of chairs on the narrow platform where the pulpit normally stood. The pulpit had been placed to the side. Amanda helped her father on to the platform and seated him in the centre chair. Reverend Davis removed two chairs while the others clumsily sorted themselves into the remaining seats. He then sat at the far left. Amanda took the seat on the far right, and, to the surprise of no one, Thad plunked down beside her.

Clarence Newton cleared his throat and then pointed to the two empty chairs. 'Levi, one of those chairs was obviously intended for Beau Haney. What about the other one?'

Reverend Davis smiled at the church's most generous

benefactor. 'I intended that chair for Deputy Rance Dehner. I wasn't sure if he'd be here or not.'

'Rance couldn't make it,' Thad spoke with a touch of mischief in his voice. 'Right now, he's busy overlooking some matters.'

The deputy turned to one side and smiled at Amanda. Still feeling giddy, Thad turned to his other side where Harry Clausen was glaring at him. The deputy stopped smiling.

Rance Dehner was back in a familiar, but not comfortable position at the top of the sycamore tree near the church. He wished this wasn't the only place to hide out and keep watch: not a good idea to use such a place twice. He had asked Harry and Thad not to mention that he had hidden in the tree on the night when they caught Otto Snider. Except for Otto, no one except the lawmen should know about it, but. . . .

The detective heard a noise coming from the wooded area behind the church. Two horsemen emerged on horseback, both dressed like the ghost of Jimmy Ellis. As they galloped towards the church one of the men pulled a Winchester from the boot of his saddle, reined in his horse and fired a shot into the sycamore tree.

Holding firm to a branch, Dehner drew his Colt and returned fire. His attacker levered the Winchester and flamed another shot into the sycamore. Dehner ducked, lost balance and plunged downward. He struggled to hold on to his six shooter as his body smashed against several branches. The tree then spat him out and Dehner landed spread-eagled on the ground.

He heard the sound of approaching hoof beats and blinked dirt from his eyes, clearing his vision. He had to gasp for breath, but he still had a hold on the gun. Rance fired a wild shot in the direction of his attacker. That move had the desired result. The hoof beats stopped and Dehner saw the image of a horse going up on its hind legs as it squealed in panic.

The detective jumped up as the rider gained control of his horse. Dehner ran behind the trunk of the tree and took two deep breaths. From inside the church he heard gunshots.

'What's that?' Levi Davis shouted.

'Guns, more than one,' Thad answered, 'And I hear horses—'

'Everyone get down!' Harry Clausen shouted as he stood up and drew his gun. Another shot sounded from outside.

People stared at each other in confusion. More gunfire could be heard.

'I said get down!' Clausen shouted again as the door to the church flew open. A man wearing the now fabled duster, hat and bandana ran inside, a pistol clutched in his right hand. 'I'm Jimmy Ellis. The real Jimmy Ellis, here for revenge.'

'Stop!' Levi Davis ran towards the middle of the platform.

A bullet scorched the air; Reverend Davis yelled in pain and staggered backwards. Harry Clausen squeezed the trigger of his six shooter. The intruder cried in pain, fired another shot at the platform, then dropped down behind the pew nearest the door.

'Do what the sheriff says, keep down,' Thad yelled as he got up and stood beside the sheriff. From what the deputy could see, everyone else on the platform was crouching near Levi Davis. The pastor appeared to be alive, although seriously hurt. They needed to get him to a doc soon.

'I'm sure I just winged the ghost,' Clausen snapped to his

deputy. 'We gotta—'

'Father!' Amanda Shaw screamed as she ran off the platform and up the aisle of the church, 'you murdered my father!'

A chorus of voices cried out to Amanda, all of them telling her to come back, all of them in vain. At the end of the aisle, the hooded figure arose from behind the last pew, like a demon ascending out of a pit of hell, and grabbed Amanda Shaw.

Rance Dehner heard more shots and screams coming from the church, but he had to remain at the trunk of the sycamore tree. He couldn't be sure of the location of his two adversaries.

His confusion didn't last long. A man's shouts sounded from in front of the church, accompanied by hoof beats. Someone was scattering most of the horses that were tethered at the hitching rail there. Rance figured one of the 'ghosts' had to be inside the church, otherwise there would be no gunshots from inside. That meant the other 'ghost' was trying to scare off the horses.

Dehner ran from the tree to the side of the church. His back against the wall and the Colt still in his hand, he advanced towards the front and glanced around the corner. A figure dressed in the outfit of Jimmy Ellis's ghost was passing by the church door. The adversary was still carrying a Winchester. He stopped at the corner of the church and looked toward the sycamore tree where he thought Dehner was still hiding.

'Throw down the rifle right now!' Dehner ordered. 'I won't say it again.'

The figure turned toward Dehner, lifting the rifle. Dehner fired and the figure staggered backwards, dropping the Winchester and stumbling to the ground.

Another hooded outlaw hastily came out of the church. In his right hand was a gun; his left arm was wrapped around the neck of Amanda Shaw. The outlaw looked about. Two horses were tied up at the hitching rail. The steeds probably belonged to Jimmy Ellis's two ghosts.

'Stay where you are!' the ghost shouted at the open door of the church. Dehner figured the sheriff and his deputy were standing right inside the doorway. The ghost then pointed his gun at the detective. 'Don't move, Dehner. It's not just you I'll kill. I'll put a bullet into the girl, too.'

Rance wanted to delay the ghost, get him talking. 'I'm surprised you know me, Jimmy. I wasn't around twenty years ago when you were hung and I don't recall us being introduced. Or maybe we were introduced, but you were using another name at the time.'

There was a bloody stain on the ghost's left shoulder. He was in no mood for conversation. 'You're a real smart guy, Dehner. Well, don't move, smart guy, or the girlie dies.'

The ghost let go of Amanda but pointed his gun directly at her and ordered her on to one of the tethered horses. As the young woman obeyed, the outlaw untied his horse from the hitching rail and mounted. Dehner noted that the hooded figure did not appear to be wobbly. He was probably losing blood, but not at a fast rate. Of course, that could change quickly.

Thad Brookshire stepped out of the church, his voice an angry shout. 'You better not hurt her!'

'That's entirely up to you and your friends, deputy,' the ghost replied. 'Don't try coming after me.'

A low moan sounded as the outlaw Dehner had shot regained consciousness. The hooded figure on the horse pumped two bullets into his comrade, then motioned with his gun hand for Amanda to ride in front of him. The two galloped away from Tin Cup together.

Dehner ran over to the fallen outlaw and ripped off his bandana. 'Beau Haney,' the detective said aloud. 'How'd he get involved in this?'

The question would have to wait. Shouting and general sounds of chaos suddenly filled the air. 'Everyone be quiet!'

Silence followed Harry Clausen's shouted order. The sheriff looked around quickly. Besides himself, Brookshire, Dehner, Lewis, and Abner Shaw were now standing outside the church.

'Abner, are you OK?' Clausen asked.

Abner Shaw lifted a shaking hand. 'Yes. I dropped to the ground, like you said, Sheriff. Amanda musta thought I got shot, she ran off. I tried yelling at her. . . .'

'We'll get her back, Abner!' Clausen had to move on, quickly. He looked at Foster Lewis. 'How's Reverend Davis doing?'

'Mr Newton and Mr Kyle are with him,' Lewis answered. 'It looks serious.'

The sheriff issued orders in a rapid fire manner. 'First, we retrieve the horses.' He looked directly at Thad. 'I want you to take off after Amanda. Use good judgment. Don't try to take on her kidnapper alone unless you have to. Leave signs along the trail so we can follow you. Only an hour or so of daylight left. If you ain't caught up to them by sundown stop and make camp. Build a fire. I'm goin' to the livery and get Stanley to look after the town while we're gone. He's done it before.'

The sheriff's eyes shifted to Dehner. 'Make sure Levi gets to the doc, and find someone to get Haney's corpse to the undertaker. I'll meet you at the doc's office and we'll take off. We shouldn't be more than twenty minutes or so behind Thad. Let's move!'

Thad Brookshire reined in his horse and looked at the sky. The sun was gone and had been for a while. The deputy knew he couldn't follow the trail left by Amanda and her abductor any longer. There wasn't enough light and his horse was tired. He had ridden him too hard.

The deputy rode at a slow gait until he came to a patch of trees that fronted a stream: a perfect place to pitch camp. He tied up his chestnut to one of the trees. Normally, he would attend to the horse first, but he needed to build a fire immediately as a signal to Sheriff Clausen and Rance Dehner. They couldn't be too far behind.

As he began to collect tinder for the fire, he wondered why the sheriff had sent him on this assignment. Both Harry Clausen and Rance Dehner were better trackers than he was.

As the fire began to ignite, the deputy suddenly realized the answer to his own question. Of course, the sheriff knew hot headed Thad Brookshire would demand to be the one to go after Amanda. Harry didn't want to waste precious time arguing with a fool kid.

For a moment, Thad crouched by the fire and stared into the flames. Their heat brought him no comfort. He hadn't been able to catch up with Amanda and her kidnapper. He wasn't completely sure he was even on their trail. He could have misread some of the signs.

Tears escaped from his eyes. Thad quickly brushed them away. He was not a child. Crying would do no good.

For a moment he thought about praying. What harm could there be in it? Reverend Davis was an intelligent, brave man and he believed in that stuff, maybe. . . .

'Thad.'

A woman's voice spoke softly to him. Thad looked over the fire to see a woman's form.

'Aren't you happy to see me, Thad?'

'Amanda!' Brookshire sprang up and ran to the woman. The couple embraced and then Thad placed a hand on each of Amanda's shoulders and held her in front of him.

'I can't believe this Amanda, how'd you escape?'

Amanda giggled like a child who had been caught pulling a naughty stunt. 'I didn't have to escape. Sheriff Clausen winged the man. He lost so much blood he passed out.'

The young woman began to laugh. She laughed much too hard for Thad.

'Are you all right, Amanda?'

'Of course, why wouldn't I be all right?'

'Who is it, Amanda? Who's the jasper who kidnapped you?'

'We don't have much time alone, Thad. Mr Dehner and Sheriff Clausen aren't far behind.'

'How do you know?'

'I looked through my field glasses a few minutes ago. There is a cloud of dust moving towards us.' The woman crumpled her face and spoke in a silly voice. 'I hereby prophesy that inside the dust clouds rides Harry Clausen and Rance Dehner.'

'Those must be powerful field glasses – to pick up a cloud of dust in the night time.'

'Look at how the moon reflects off the water.'

Thad continued to hold on to the woman as he turned his head. Something was very wrong, but he didn't know what. 'You're right,' he said with a fake cheerfulness. 'It's very pretty.'

'Let's go have a closer look.'

The couple began to walk, hand in hand, to the creek. Thad felt increasingly nervous. He tried to figure out Amanda's strange behaviour. A sudden thought sent a shock through his already ragged emotions. Had the kidnapper violated Amanda? Was she. . . .

They arrived at the water's edge. Amanda looked down at the light reflecting in the stream. 'Nature is strange, isn't it?'

'What do you mean?'

The woman looked up into the sky. 'Nature can be so beautiful from afar. But up close, it's so cruel. The heat dries up the water, animals die, people die. Folks come here from the east seeking a dream. They rarely find it. Life in the west is hard, very hard.'

Thad couldn't think of what to say. He settled for, 'You sound like you're sad.'

Amanda turned and faced Thad. 'I'm happy when I'm with you.'

She took a step towards him. Thad put his arms around the woman and pressed her against him as they kissed. In that moment, Thad knew he could never leave this woman. Whatever had happened to her, whatever stood behind her melancholy, she was the woman he wanted by his side for the rest of his life.

The couple gradually released each other and Amanda took a short step backwards. 'You're a good man, Thad. A good man.'

The deputy laughed softly. 'Well, thank you ma'am, you're pretty nice yourself.'

She gently ran a hand over his face. 'I wish I could be nice, I wish I could be Amanda Shaw.'

This time, the deputy's laughter was forced. 'You've been hearing too much talk about ghosts. You are Amanda Shaw.'

Amanda's face took on a pleading quality as if she wanted

Thad to understand something important about herself. 'There are two Amandas. The nice Amanda that I pretend to be most of the time and the real Amanda.'

Thad respected the woman's apparent agony. His voice was quiet and held no mockery. 'And what is the real Amanda like?'

She smiled and tilted her head slightly in a wistful manner. 'I'm a cold blooded killer.' She took the gun from the deputy's holster and pointed it at his head. 'You're going to do exactly what I say, Thad, or I'll kill you.'

The woman's laugh was playful, but Thad saw the madness in her eyes.

CHAPTER NINETEEN

Harry Clausen and Rance Dehner reined up and stared at the dying red light which emanated from a spot beside a grove of trees. 'Looks like someone started a fire for a camp, but had a change of heart,' Dehner said.

'Doesn't make sense,' Clausen spoke as a couple of small sparks shot up from the embers and quickly vanished into the night. 'Let's check it out, careful like. This could be a trap.'

The two men dismounted and grounded their horses' reins with stones. They palmed their guns and moved cautiously towards the abandoned camp.

They paused for a few moments and looked around. Satisfied that there was no danger nearby, they holstered their weapons. Both men carefully examined the only partially doused campfire.

'Someone was pretty anxious to take off, or else someone wanted us to know he'd been here,' the sheriff said.

'And someone wanted to leave a clue,' Dehner picked up a bullet that lay just outside the fire's glow and handed it to Clausen.

'This could be from Thad's gun belt,' Clausen speculated. 'Maybe Amanda's kidnapper spotted Thad. Knew he was on his trail. He tied Amanda up, then rode back and waited. . . .'

'I'm not so sure our so-called kidnapper had to tie Amanda up.'

The sheriff looked confused. 'Whaddya mean?'

Dehner stared into the dying embers. He had postponed this moment as long as he could. Too long probably. 'Harry, I think Amanda may be deeply involved in this whole Jimmy Ellis matter.'

'What?! Oh hell, I've known Amanda since before she could walk—'

'Just hear me out,' Rance began pacing about. 'Amanda has a motive. It's general knowledge that the Rocking S is in trouble. Abner Shaw is not the man he once was, his mind seems to be going, but he still insists on running the ranch. He's running it into the ground. Amanda will probably inherit the ranch someday by that time, though, it may be worthless.'

The sheriff shook his head. 'I still don't see how—'

'If Abner Shaw were to die mysteriously, Amanda would be a prime suspect. But, if the ghost of Jimmy Ellis were to return to Tin Cup and kill off the men who hung him, no one would give a thought to Amanda being the culprit.'

'That's one damn crazy theory. You got any evidence?'

'Some,' Dehner kept his voice calm, ignoring Harry

Clausen's obvious anger. 'From what I could tell, Art Sherman's body wasn't carried to that cottonwood where Jimmy Ellis was hung. Sherman was shot to death right there. I suspect the same thing happened to Jed Coogan.'

'But why in hell would those two men ride out to a line shack on the Rocking S ranch?'

'Because they thought they were riding out to a rendezvous with a very beautiful young woman.'

Harry Clausen's face went ashen.

'Everybody knows Amanda is good at baking,' Rance continued, 'I suspect that's how she made her initial contact. Taking a pie to the ranchers. I know Jed Coogan was a widower, but he'd probably have been embarrassed if anyone had known he was keeping company with a girl young enough to be his daughter.'

'Sherman was a married man,' Clausen added, 'and arrogant as hell. He'd think nothing about. . . .' The lawman didn't finish. He didn't have to.

The sheriff took off his hat and wiped his brow. There was little heat coming from the dying fire, but even so Harry Clausen was sweating. 'Damn it all, Rance, Amanda Shaw couldn't have just kidnapped herself!' Dehner nodded. 'I'm sure Amanda has an accomplice: Leo Jensen. The girl has probably promised Leo she'll marry him in exchange for his cooperation.'

'How'd you figure Jensen is tied up in it?' The anger had gone from the sheriff's voice, replaced by a deep sorrow.

'That run-in Leo had with Thad at the early morning picnic, it was phony. Think about it. Leo Jensen is not the type of man who gives up on a fight after taking only one punch.'

'But why?'

'Amanda is a very smart lady,' Dehner answered as he

continued to pace. 'She knew no one would suspect her in the whole Jimmy Ellis matter, but they might take a careful look at Leo. Especially Thad, since the two men didn't exactly get along. Once the law suspected Leo, no telling where the investigation would go—'

'I still don't understand the phony fight.'

'Before the fight, Leo went into a story about Abner Shaw telling his daughter she didn't want him seeing a lawman. Then, Amanda thanked Leo for being kind to her father, for staying up late with him that night and listening to his army stories. Remember all of this presumably happened on the night Art Sherman was gunned down. Amanda was handing Leo an alibi for the night of the murder. And right in front of Thad, the man who'd be most likely to suspect him! Since we assumed the same person killed both Sherman and Coogan, Leo was off the hook.'

Harry Clausen stared down at the embers, now more gray than red. 'Amanda was the one who set up the meetin' with that crazy writer. I'll bet she talked poor Abner into it. And she set it up so's Abner was sittin' right in the middle of the church, where he'd be an easy target.'

Dehner stopped pacing and faced the sheriff directly. 'That's why I insisted both you and Thad be at that meeting while I stood guard outside. I should have told you my theory then, but the evidence was so circumstantial.'

'I wouldn't have believed you anyhow. I shoulda been more alert. Thad, too. Reverend Davis paid for our mistakes. I sure hope he's gonna be OK.'

Dehner hastily pulled the sheriff back to the present. 'I don't see any signs of a struggle. I think Amanda came here, not Leo.'

Clausen sighed deeply. 'If what you reckon is true, Amanda was willin' to kill five men along with killin' her own father. Amanda Shaw is a monster.'

'Yes, and right now Thad is in the hands of that monster.'

CHAPTER TWENTY

Thad Brookshire had never liked mountains. Something about the height and the thin air gave him a headache. He had a very bad headache now, but it had little to do with the air and everything to do with the gun pressing hard against his backbone.

'Stop right here!' The feminine voice still sounded playful, almost flirtatious.

The climb had opened on to a plateau, with a cave that even a man well over six feet could enter without ducking his head. Thad quickly glanced upwards. Friends had told him the stars and moon shone brighter in the mountains because you were closer to heaven. Thad reckoned the lights might be brighter, but he felt a far distance from heaven.

'You carry matches don't you?'

'Yes.' Thad answered his captor.

'Very slowly take a match out of your pocket and light it with your thumb. Don't do anything silly!' Amanda had ordered Thad not to be silly several times. On each occasion, he realized how little his life meant to a woman who, despite everything, he still loved.

Thad followed instructions; a match flared in his right hand.

'Step inside the cave. Move slowly.'

The match threw a glimmer of light on to the cave wall. The pinpoint of brightness moved beside them like a firefly winging through the darkness of hades. Amanda called out: 'Leo, honey, can you hear me?'

'Yep,' The reply was not too distant.

'I'm bringing a guest.'

The woman's voice went lower. 'The cave takes a twist up ahead. Just follow it.'

Thad continued to obey orders and was soon entering a huge cavern with a fire that illuminated a large patch of space. Standing in the middle of that patch was Leo Jensen. The hatred Thad had seen on Jensen's face so many times before was there, accompanied by a glint of cocky amusement in his eyes.

'Well, well. Hello, deputy.' Before Jensen stepped away from the fire, Thad could see that the ramrod's left shoulder had been bandaged. Jensen swaggered toward the deputy in a threatening manner. Thad blew out the almost burned up match stick and tossed it to the ground, freeing his right arm.

The gun pressed harder against his back. 'Don't move,' Amanda whispered.

Thad could do nothing, but brace himself for the blow that slammed against the side of his face. The deputy plunged to the ground.

Jensen hovered over him, shaking a fist. 'You damn fool! You think you can best me in a fight?'

The deputy stared upwards at his enemy. 'I can beat you in a fair fight, Jensen. Of course, when you rely on a woman to keep a gun on me that does change the odds.'

Jensen took a step backwards. 'Get up! I'll show you—'

'No Leo, not right now,' Amanda's voice was beseeching. 'You're hurt—'

'Not much,' Jensen cut her off. 'The bullet didn't touch a bone. It didn't even do much damage, just ripped some skin.'

'But you've lost blood, Leo. Wait until you've regained all your strength. Besides, we've got important work to do . . . important for our future together.'

Amanda ran a hand across Leo's face as she had done with Thad less than two hours before. She took a quick step towards the ramrod. Their bodies came together in a natural, familiar manner as they kissed. Thad felt sick.

But he didn't have to watch the embrace for long. Amanda backed away from Leo, gave him a smile, a wink, and Thad's .44. She then looked down at the deputy.

'Now you understand why Leo always held you in contempt. My playing up to you was the one part of our scheme that Leo didn't much care for. Leo still hates you, Thad. Better not forget that. Let's move closer to the fire.'

Thad took a careful look around as he returned to his feet. A Henry lay at the far edge of the fire's light. There appeared to be only one way out of the cave, the way they had come in, though several large boulders stood on all sides except where they had entered. The light in the cavern wasn't good enough to even take a guess as to what was on the other side of those boulders. Maybe. . . .

Amanda read his mind. 'Don't even think about escaping.' She pointed a finger towards the fire. 'Move.'

Thad led the way with the gun no longer pressed against his back, but still close enough. When they arrived beside the blaze, Amanda ordered him to sit down. Leo sat down nearby. Their backs were to the cave entrance. The deputy noted that Leo looked wan, but not seriously wounded. In a few days, he would be fine.

Amanda remained on her feet. She picked up a canteen

and handed it to the ramrod. 'Drink up, Leo. You need to get back that lost blood.' She smiled at Thad. 'Leo doesn't look after his health very well. I have to do it for him. That old saying is true. All men are really just little boys.'

Thad couldn't tell if the woman was serious or taunting him. He said nothing.

'Leo, I think you should tell Thad how you came to know about this cave.'

The ramrod gave Thad an arrogant smirk. 'An outlaw is always looking for a good hide out. I usta have me a gang. We'd meet here, and I'd explain the set-up. We'd do the job, ride back here and split up the loot. Then we'd set a date to meet here in this cave and go our separate ways for 'bout four months. In between times, I'd work on a ranch. A jasper hanging around town playing cards and drinking all day is likely to interest the law.'

'How many robberies have you pulled?' Thad asked.

'Three,' Jensen replied. 'Had one more planned. Can't use the same hide out too much. The law will wise up. The last job went good. We held up a Wells Fargo stage. We was going to meet just once more and—'

'Take another drink of water, Leo.' Amanda's voice was soft but she was still giving an order.

Leo complied and then continued: 'But two of my gang got greedy. They tried to pull a bank robbery by themselves over in Platt. The sheriff there killed both of them. Stupid jackasses, never could do anything on their own.'

Thad wanted to keep the conversation going until he could devise a plan. 'What happened to the third member of the gang?'

Leo handed the canteen back to Amanda who corked it and placed it on the ground. 'He turned yellow,' Leo said. 'Went straight. Used the money from the Wells Fargo hold up to start him a farm somewhere.'

Amanda sighed loudly, 'Money can do strange things to a man.'

'Ain't that the truth!' Leo smiled at Thad Brookshire, a broad, cruel smile. 'But it all worked out just fine. While working at the Rocking S, I met Amanda and found out we got a lot in common. A lot. One of those things: we both wanna be rich.'

'And we're going to be rich,' Amanda's voice once again sounded girlish and joyful. 'Leo knows this area like the back of his hand and he still has friends he met while pulling robberies. And Thad, you are going to help us get rich.'

'I'm not going to help you! And you can forget your dreams about living in a mansion. The law will catch up with you. Both of you!'

Amanda's laughter filled the cave. She was having fun. 'We won't get caught! This has all been so easy! I had no trouble at all getting Jed Coogan and Art Sherman out to the line shack. All I really had to do was smile at them . . . in a certain way.'

A look of whimsy came into the woman's face as she thought back on two murders. 'I felt a bit sorry for Jed. He was gruff, but still a nice man. But Art Sherman, what a puffed up fool! You should have seen the expression on his face when he turned and saw me holding a gun on him. And when I shot him. . . .'

The woman's laughter became sharp and laced with madness. Thad wondered if soon the woman would be talking about him in a manner similar to how she mentioned Jed Coogan: *Thad was really a sweet guy. Too bad I had to put a bullet through his skull.*

Leo Jensen saw the despair on Thad's face. He wanted to push it deeper. 'Amanda, tell our guest 'bout our little charade at the line shack.'

Amanda gave Jensen an affectionate smile. The affection became mockery when she looked at their prisoner. 'I had Leo dig up that hole behind the line shack to make it look like Jimmy Ellis had clawed his way out of the grave. Leo didn't like the idea. He thought it went too far. He may have been right.' She shifted her gaze back to her colleague. 'Leo's usually right.'

The woman looked down in a shy gesture, then again eyed Thad. 'Of course, it was Leo dressed up like the ghost of Jimmy Ellis who fired at us that night I got you to the line shack. Remember when we chased the ghost back to the ranch?'

Thad sighed. 'Yes, I remember.'

A playful expression returned to Amanda's eyes. 'I led you on a long way back to the ranch. Leo had plenty of time to get back and hide behind the tool shed. I told you I saw someone in front of the ranch house.' The woman giggled. 'I lied. Leo and I had it all planned out. Even the part about him acting jealous of you.'

Thad gave a low moan. Jensen responded with short laughs that sounded like barks. 'What's wrong, deputy? Not feeling so good?'

Thad looked directly at Amanda. 'Rance told me to not tell anybody he had been hiding in a tree on the night of the temperance meeting, but I told you. I even told you Rance would be back in that tree today.'

'That's right, deputy,' Leo said, 'and Amanda told me all 'bout it. That's why I got Beau Haney to keep Dehner occupied. I'd already scared the old souse plenty in my ghost outfit. Got him to spread the word about Jimmy Ellis. Of course, I knew I'd have to kill him when it was all done. I think he was starting to figure out who I really was.'

Anger flared in Thad's voice as he faced Amanda. 'When Leo broke into the church, you grabbed my arm. I thought you cared about me. You were protecting Leo as much as you could. You probably hoped he'd kill the others. Really build up the Jimmy Ellis legend.'

'Yes,' Amanda agreed. 'But things went crazy. Harry Clausen winged Leo with his first shot and . . . how could I know that preacher would stop a bullet in order to protect my father?'

A look of confusion fell over Amanda's face and she looked vulnerable. 'I never understood Levi Davis. Sometimes he looks at me like all men look at me, but he's different. And today he ruined our plan. You see, Leo was going to kill Father. I was going to scream and run at him. Leo would take me as a hostage and keep the law at bay. The law would find me and I'd tell them I had escaped. I'd inherit the ranch, sell it, and meet Leo in California.'

'Didn't quite work out.' Leo spoke as he moved the .44 closer to Thad. 'But we got us another plan and that's where you come in, Deputy.'

'What do you mean?' Thad asked.

'Your daddy is one of the wealthiest men in Texas.' Overwhelming joy replaced the confusion on Amanda's face. 'And he will pay plenty to get his son back.'

'You're crazy!'

Thad's shout did nothing to impede Amanda's joy. She continued to speak. 'You are going to write a letter to your father, telling him when and where to deliver twenty-five thousand dollars in cash.'

'How are you going to mail the letter? How are you going to keep out of sight until you get the money? How do you—'

'Let us worry about the details, Thad,' Amanda said. 'All you have to do is write the letter. Co-operate, and after we collect the money, we'll turn you loose before we disappear.'

Thad's efforts at coming up with a clever plan for escape were getting nowhere. He was in a strange location with a gun being pointed at him. Most disorienting: the woman he loved had transformed in front of him and become a demon, giddy over her ability to kill. His mind was scrambled. He decided on a desperate gambit: an old ploy that might work. First, he needed to set up his captors.

'You two sure had me fooled,' Thad spoke in a resigned manner. 'But there's one thing I don't understand.'

'What's that?' Amanda looked delighted over Thad's admission.

'You want to get rid of your father and get control of the Rocking S, right?'

'Right!' The woman replied.

'That being the case, it seems to me you two failed. People are going to notice Leo Jensen not being around. They're going to nail him as the ghost of Jimmy Ellis. I suppose you could go back, Amanda and tell people you escaped—'

The woman didn't want the captor to go on. 'That's not going to happen! I've given up on the ranch. After your father gives us the twenty-five thousand, Leo and I are heading far away from here.'

Thad laughed and tried to make it sound genuine. 'Just what I wanted to you to say. There's a posse of men right behind you. I wanted them to hear the whole truth.'

Both Leo and Amanda looked backwards. Thad jumped Leo and delivered a rabbit punch to the outlaw's nose. Leo bellowed in pain. His arm reflexively shot out. The .44 twirled from his hand and landed about three feet away.

Thad disconnected from the outlaw and scrambled on his

knees toward the weapon. He had just picked up the gun when something hard rammed against the back of his head. Red clouds began to dance around him in the darkness. He was hit again. The deputy fell over unconscious.

Drops of blood landed on Thad's back as Leo bent over and yanked the .44 out of the deputy's hand. 'That damn snake, I outta—' Leo moved one leg back getting ready to land a kick into Thad's ribs.

'Don't, Leo, it won't do any good!' Amanda tossed down the rock she had used as a weapon. 'I need to bandage his head. We'll let him sleep for a few hours. He needs to be able to think straight. He has to write that letter to his rich daddy.'

'And what if he keeps saying no?'

Amanda pointed at the fire. 'Remember our plan?'

Leo pressed his lips together and tried to hide his humiliation at needing help to bring down Thad. 'Yep, but now I'm gonna do things a little different.'

'What do you mean, honey?'

'Before we even ask rich boy to write the letter, I'm gonna give him one good, long burn. Let him know what he's in for if he holds out.'

Amanda knew she had to go along with Leo Jensen. She needed him, for the moment. 'Sure honey, but don't hold the flame to him too long.'

'Why not?'

Amanda's voice again became girlish and playful. 'Why, burning flesh just smells something awful.'

CHAPTER TWENTY-ONE

Rance Dehner opened his eyes, shattering the nightmarish images which had tormented his sleep. The past always catches up with you at night, he thought. You can keep it at bay as long as your eyes are open, but when you sleep . . . he immediately vanquished the pictures of a dying girl from his mind. That was the past. That was gone forever. This new day would bring a load of new problems. That seemed to be the way it always worked.

The detective looked upwards. Light was beginning to edge out the darkness, but only beginning. He glanced sideways. Harry Clausen had reignited the fire and had set up a spider web over it; a coffee pot hung on the web. Clausen was sipping on a cup. He appeared lost in thought.

Dehner jumped to his feet. He had slept with his boots on for, he reckoned, about three hours. He doubted if Harry Clausen had slept at all.

'Can you share some of that java?' Dehner asked.

Clausen stooped over, then righted himself and handed Dehner an empty cup across the fire. 'I won't charge you nothin' if you promise not to complain about the coffee.'

Dehner took the cup. He knew that was the last small talk he'd hear from Harry Clausen on this day. Rance took another quick look at the sky. 'We should be able to start tracking them pretty soon.'

'I'm not sure trackin' them is the best idea.'

Dehner gave his colleague a curious stare.

'I've been thinkin' on somethin' Beau Haney told me back in the days when he was a good lawman. Beau said when you're after outlaws, always remember the two w's: women and water.'

The sheriff gave Dehner a cockeyed smile and continued. 'Beau let the girls in the saloons know that if they picked up any information on some varmint, he'd pay 'em for it. Felt it was a good use of the town's money. I've nabbed a few no-goods myself that way. You'd be surprised how much a drunken owlhoot will spill to a lady of the evenin'.'

Dehner poured himself a cup of coffee and returned the pot to the spider web. 'What about the other w?'

The smile vanished from Clausen's face. 'You can't go long without water. And I'm sure I shot Jenkins back at the church: another reason he'll be needin' water.'

Dehner blew gently on his coffee. 'So?'

'There have been three big robberies in this area over the last year or so, none of them in Tin Cup, so investigatin' those robberies involved questions of jurisdiction and all that.'

Clausen took another sip of java, then continued. 'The last job was a doozy. The gunneys held up a Wells Fargo stage at just the right time. Got away with a lot of loot. I got up a posse. We trailed the gang into the mountains and lost them there.'

Dehner stared at the massive dark outline which blocked the coming light of day. A line of ragged cliffs made the mountain range look like a mythical dragon. 'Tracking someone in all that hard rock will be tough.' He let go of an anxiety that had been plaguing him since they found the deserted camp site. 'Leo and Amanda may have taken Thad up there somewhere, it'll be rough.'

'Maybe not!'

Dehner's eyebrows jumped.

'I couldn't spend much time lookin' for those stagecoach robbers,' the sheriff explained. 'I have a town to look after. But I got to thinkin' what Beau Haney told me years ago.' Clausen nodded his head towards the mountain range. 'Those mountains are pretty dry. Don't know why. But the east end is different. There's a large stream that runs along there.'

Harry paused for a moment and gulped down a deluge of coffee. 'One day I rode back up on those mountains and followed the green. Found a cave, a very big cave. Sure enough, someone had been there. There were the remains of a fire. I'm pretty sure it was the owlhoots who pulled the Wells Fargo hold-up.'

Dehner realized where this was heading. 'You think Leo Jensen was one of the stage coach robbers?'

'Yep,' Clausen shot back. 'Something 'bout that jasper has never seemed right with me. Talked some with Abner. Found out Jensen had taken a week off when the Wells Fargo job was pulled. Can't jail a man for that. Still, I say we check out that cave before we do anything else.'

'I agree.'

'Finish up your coffee, Rance. It may be the last thing you put in your stomach for a while.'

CHAPTER TWENTY-TWO

Dawn dominated the sky and provided adequate light as the two lawmen rode up a mountain trail. Harry Clausen took the lead. He had been in these mountains before.

A horse nickered in the distance. Both men dismounted and led their mounts upwards until they came to a collection of huge boulders interspersed with green growth.

Behind the boulders was a downward slope that ran for several yards and collided with a stream. Nine scrawny tress were bunched by the water, and sided by a large boulder. Three unsaddled horses were tied to the trees.

'Looks like some folks planned to stay a while,' Harry Clausen spoke in a low voice.

The sheriff and his deputy slowly walked their horses to the stream and allowed them to drink, then tied them up on one of the trees. Dehner pulled a Winchester from the boot on the saddle of his bay. The sheriff looked upwards in the direction of the cave. 'Let's hope they're still sleepin', that way we can—'

A horrifying bellow of pain cut off the sheriff's words. 'That's Thad!' Clausen's voice was frantic. 'I'm sure of it.'

Dehner touched his friend's arm lightly. 'We've got to move fast, but move quiet. We won't be much help to Thad if they hear us coming.'

Harry nodded his head. He was once again the experienced lawman. He led Rance up the slope and to the cave entrance. The sheriff struck a match and continued to lead the way as the two lawmen entered cautiously, making little noise on the cave's soft ground. Harry held up one hand and stopped where the cave took a turn. Both men paused and listened.

Leo Jensen was laughing, but when he spoke his voice conveyed rage not humour. 'I almost hope you don't write the letter, rich boy. You know what I'd enjoy more than twenty-five thousand dollars from your daddy? I'd love to burn you to death, a few inches at a time.'

'You're being used, Leo.' Thad's voice sounded strong and lucid.

'What are you talking about?' Leo shot back.

'Amanda. She's going to use you like she used me. When she gets her hands on that twenty-five thousand, she won't need you anymore. Truth is, you'll be a burden to her. She's going to kill you and—'

A woman's voice cried out: 'He's lying Leo, don't listen to anything he says. He's lying.'

Clausen and Dehner exchanged knowing glances. They now had a fair idea of the location of everyone in the cave. And 'fair' was as good as it was going to get.

The sheriff tossed aside the match and drew his six shooter. Both lawmen took several quick strides around the turn in the cave. 'Freeze, all of you!' Clausen shouted.

Thad Brookshire's shirt was off and his hands were tied behind his back. He was sitting near the fire with his back to the entrance. Leo Jensen stood over him holding a flaming torch.

Dehner spotted a shadow moving in the darkness near the fire. He pushed Clausen down and hit the ground himself as a bullet whistled over them and ricocheted off a stone wall.

Jensen dropped the torch into the fire and moved out of the light. Whispered voices could be heard but neither lawman could make out what they were saying. Amanda seemed to be doing most of the talking.

Jensen shouted out, 'Throw down your guns or I'll kill rich boy.'

The detective was sure Jensen was acting on orders from Amanda Shaw. Dehner reckoned the lady was not about to kill a hostage worth twenty-five thousand dollars. He could hear the swishing of cautious footsteps. Jensen was moving, probably behind a large rock. The outlaw wasn't going to allow his voice to betray his location.

Rance thought he heard other footsteps moving quietly in a different direction, towards the cave entrance. But he couldn't be sure and there was no time to think on it.

Dehner gripped his Winchester and shouted. 'You're bluffing, Leo. I don't believe you.'

'Here's something to think about, Dehner!' Jensen rose from behind the rock where he had taken cover and fired a shot that landed near Thad. Rance fired in the direction of the orange flame. Jensen cried out in pain. A metallic sound pinged twice in the darkness. Jensen's rifle hitting rock as it tumbled to the cave floor.

Several moments of silence followed. Thad broke the stillness as he shouted, 'I think Jensen is dead. I can see his arm. It's not moving. Good shooting. Leo fired a warning shot at me to scare you. He had to make it as close as he could. Leo always was a show-off.'

Harry Clausen returned the shout. 'Do you know where Amanda is?'

'No. But she has my .44. She's the one that fired at you first.'

Clausen shouted again. 'Amanda Shaw, drop the gun and

step into the firelight with both hands up.'

Stillness once again pervaded the cave. No sounds bounced about the rock enclosure. The sheriff grimaced, and raised his voice once again. 'This is your last chance to surrender peaceable, Amanda. Step into the light with—'

A gunshot decimated the quiet. Thad gave a loud screech.

'She shot him!' Clausen yelled as he started to get back on to his feet.

Dehner pulled the sheriff back to the ground. 'Stay low.'

'We've got to get to Thad!'

'You're not going to do him any good if you get shot yourself!' There was a pleading quality in Dehner's loud whisper.

'He could be bleedin'—'

'OK! Give me a second.' Dehner shouted out: 'Amanda, I'm carrying a Winchester which has a lot more punch than that .44 you have. We're going to help Thad; if you fire on us, you'll end up like Leo Jensen.'

Thad cried out that he was OK and for the lawmen to stay where they were. Otherwise, there was no sound.

'Stay behind me,' Rance said to the sheriff. 'Amanda's aim probably won't be all that good in this dark cave.'

Dehner hoped he was right. This was a bad plan, but Harry Clausen was determined to get to Thad. The detective couldn't stop him.

Both men sprang to their feet and moved forwards in jackknife positions. Dehner shielded Clausen by moving beside him facing the direction where Amanda's shot had come from.

Thad again cried out for Clausen and Dehner to stay where they were. Under Thad's shout, the detective thought he heard footsteps moving stealthily out of the cave, but he couldn't be certain.

When they reached Thad, the young man's face was covered by perspiration. There was a burn under his ribs on the left side, but it wasn't too bad. For all his harsh bravado, Leo Jensen had been following Amanda's orders.

Both Dehner and Clausen crouched low, in front of Thad. Dehner continued to look for Amanda. He had his Winchester ready.

'Are you OK, boy?' Clausen asked anxiously.

'I'm fine. Amanda's shot missed me, but not by much. It scared me plenty and I howled like a lonesome coyote. Sorry. I've made a real mess of things.'

'Don't worry, boy, you done fine. . . .'

Dehner hastily turned his head to face his colleagues. 'Check on Jensen.' The detective immediately shifted his eyes back to the area where Amanda could be hiding.

Thad nodded his head to the left. 'Over there.'

Clausen duck walked over to where an arm protruded from a large rock. He felt for a pulse as he glanced at the rest of the body. 'Dead. Jensen won't be causin' us no more trouble.'

Dehner waited until the sheriff did his duck walk back before he addressed the two men in a low voice. 'I think Amanda has gone. I'm going after her. You two be careful, I might be wrong. She could be hiding just about anywhere in this cave, waiting for a chance to shoot us down.'

Rance followed his own advice. He moved out of the cave cautiously, alert to any sound that might betray where an ambusher could be lying in wait.

Outside, the sun was now bright. The detective paused for a moment and allowed his eyes to adjust, then headed for the most likely place Amanda would flee.

Dehner ran until he reached the area where the two lawmen had tied up their horses. He paused at top of the incline and looked over a large rock at the horses tethered near the stream. One horse was gone: Clausen's roan, which already had a saddle on it. That made sense. Amanda would ride off on a saddled horse.

The detective ducked down behind the rock. Amanda Shaw was a smart woman who would not panic. She would be carefully thinking through her options. The woman knew Leo Jensen was out of commission. Her deception had been uncovered and there was nothing to stop the law from coming after her.

Would she try to run? Maybe not. Chances are she'd be caught.

But if the woman could dispose of Clausen, Dehner and Thad she could concoct some tale about being kidnapped and the three lawmen being killed while rescuing her. Despite the circumstances, Dehner chuckled to himself as he imagined Amanda Shaw relating the story. There wasn't a soul in town she wouldn't convince.

Rance once again peered over the rock. He thought he heard a branch rustle in the trees. Clausen's roan could be somewhere in that grove feasting on leaves.

From behind the boulder that ended the row of trees, the detective thought he saw sunlight glint off . . . something . . . probably Thad's .44. Dehner decided on a course of action which he knew was foolish. But he also knew it was a plan he had to try.

Rance was now reasonably certain Amanda was behind the boulder near the horses. He didn't think she had spotted him. The detective gripped his Winchester hard and moved swiftly down the incline towards the horses. He hoped the brim of his hat would at least partially cover his eyes which were fixed on the boulder. He saw Amanda's blonde head first before he saw the gun come into view.

Dehner dropped to the ground a moment before Amanda fired two shots. He could only hope she wouldn't notice. He screamed in phony pain and tossed the Winchester down the slope far out of reach. He hoped that action would convince Amanda her shots had hit their target and provide him with a ploy.

Amanda Shaw stepped slowly and cautiously from behind the boulder, .44 in hand. She quickly assessed the situation. Rance Dehner was lying on his face about halfway down the incline. The Winchester had tumbled several feet away from him and was now about as close to her as it was to the detective.

That rifle was valuable. She could use it to finish off Dehner if necessary and it would be a real help in killing the sheriff and Thad.

There were only two bullets left in the .44. She had to be careful and not waste ammunition. But she couldn't be slow. Clausen might have heard the shots.

Keeping the .44 pointed at Dehner, Amanda scampered toward the Winchester. She hastily bent over and picked it up. Grasping the rifle in her left hand, she smilingly admired it.

The admiration cost her. Dehner drew his pistol and fired two shots near the woman's feet. Amanda raised both arms as if creating a shield, stumbled backwards and then toppled over. She quickly got on to one knee and pointed the .44 at Dehner. The Winchester was still in her left hand.

Dehner now stood only a few feet away from the woman, his weapon still smoking. 'Throw down the guns, Miss Shaw!'

'Mr Dehner, Leo Jensen forced me to—'

'Throw down the guns, Miss Shaw!'

Amanda Shaw stared long and carefully at the man

standing over her. A sly smile crossed her face, 'You wouldn't shoot a woman.'

Dehner pulled back the hammer on his .45. 'Maybe if Thad Brookshire were standing here, you'd be right. Thad may have a few grains of idealism left in him, despite what you've done. But I lost that long ago. I won't hesitate to put a bullet in the head of a woman who has killed two men, tried to kill her own father, and seduced another man into torture. I'll say this once more: throw down the guns, Miss Shaw!'

Miss Shaw threw down the guns.

Dehner ordered the woman on to her feet. He walked her over to his bay, pulled handcuffs from his saddle-bags and cuffed the woman's hands behind her back. As he did so, the detective observed an unusual phenomenon. Tears were streaking down her face. Nothing odd about that, but Amanda's face blazed anger. The tears were tears of rage – aimed at what?

Dehner figured he would never know the answer to that question, or another question he had. For the rest of his days, as he sat alone beside a campfire, Rance Dehner would occasionally think back on the remarkable beauty of Amanda Shaw and wonder if he could ever have kept his word and fired a bullet into such a lovely face.

CHAPTER TWENTY-THREE

Harry Clausen felt tense as he skimmed over the paperwork on his desk. The threesome that suddenly stormed into his office did nothing for the lawman's disposition. There were three ladies, all with mouths pressed into a straight line, all very active in the temperance movement. This was not going to be pleasant.

The sheriff rose, smiled at his visitors and tried to sound cordial. 'Mrs Duffy, Mrs Peterson and Mrs Albright, it's a pleasure to—'

'We're here to talk to you about a scandal you are creating in this town, Sheriff!' The speaker was Elmira Duffy, who was obviously speaking for the group.

Clausen suspected what this was all about and tried to establish a light, friendly mood. 'Mrs Duffy, I'm afraid I'm long past the age where I can stir up a scandal.'

Elmira was not amused. 'We're not here to indulge in coarse humour, Sheriff. We know that you have a young lady in prison and she is sharing a cell with a male prisoner!'

'That's not true!' Clausen declared. 'Right now, I have three cells and two prisoners. Each prisoner is in a separate cell. One side of Amanda Shaw's cell faces a wall, the other side faces the cell which holds Otto Snider. I have hung a blanket across the side of that cell to protect Miss Shaw's . . . privacy.'

'Some privacy!' Elmira shouted. 'Is the front of the cell covered?'

'No.'

'So, the lawmen can gawp at her any time they please!'

'Lawmen don't gawp!' Clausen retorted.

The sheriff took a deep breath. He was letting Elmira get to him. He had always believed in staying calm in the face of adversity and this was certainly adversity. 'Look, ladies, this has been hard on all of us. In the entire time I've packed a star in Tin Cup, I've never jailed a woman. But Amanda Shaw stands accused of murder and attempted murder.'

'I will remind you, Sheriff, that Miss Shaw is innocent until proven guilty in a court of law.'

'You don't have to remind me of that, Mrs Duffy.' Clausen had now regained his composure. 'When we brought Amanda Shaw in five days ago, I contacted the authorities in Dallas, where there is a women's prison. A United States Marshall is arrivin' early this afternoon to escort Miss Shaw to Dallas. She'll probably stand trial there.'

Elmira seemed to lose a bit of her starch, but she still wanted to finish on a strong note. 'Rest assured we will be here this afternoon to ensure that your woman prisoner is treated in a humane and proper manner!'

'I look forward to seein' you then.' Clausen managed to hold the sarcasm in his voice to a slight undertone.

The three ladies marched out of the office, almost colliding with Stanley Abbot, who was starting to enter. The hostler took off his hat and leaned against the doorway until the women had departed. He closed the door behind him and smirked as he approached the Sheriff. 'What would that be all 'bout?'

'It's too complicated to explain right now.'

Abbot looked behind him as if fearing that the threesome

would charge back in. 'Yep, it did look sorta . . . complee-cated.' The livery owner was a medium-sized, stout man with tobacco-stained fingers and teeth. A few strands of straw clung to his checkered shirt.

'I appreciate you watchin' the office for an hour or so, Stanley.' Clausen pointed to a Winchester on his desk. 'In case you need it. Don't think you will. The prisoners have been pretty quiet of late.' The sheriff walked to the front door. He tossed Stanley a wave and a 'Help yourself to the coffee,' as he exited.

Walking along the boardwalk, the sheriff whispered to himself, 'Elmira and her crew have a point. I'll be glad when the marshal arrives.'

But as he made his way towards the Beecher Hotel, Clausen mused on the real reason he wanted Amanda Shaw out of town. These last few days had been hard on Thad. The boy had withdrawn into himself, doing his job conscientiously, but saying little. Having a girl he once loved and maybe still did love, sitting in a jail cell could only be adding to the young man's agony.

Harry Clausen slowed his pace. Was this scheme of his really such a good idea? Would it help Thad get on with his life and his job as a lawman or would it make things worse? Thad had only nodded his head when he presented the idea to him. Rance Dehner seemed more enthusiastic.

When Clausen had told the ladies in his office about wiring Dallas concerning his female prisoner, he didn't mention that he had also sent a wire to the *Dallas Herald.* A reporter for the Herald was sitting on a chair in front of the Beecher Hotel as the lawman approached it.

'I hope your room is as good as I told you it would be when you stepped off the stagecoach, Mr Harland.' The sheriff tried to keep the anxiety out of his voice.

Jim Harland was a tall, skinny man with thick brown hair. He smiled as he stood up. 'The room is fine, Sheriff. I've covered a lot of territory for the *Herald* and spent a lot of time dozing by a campfire. Some men think sleeping under the stars is romantic. Some men are loco. I'll take a hotel room anytime I can get it.'

The lawman nodded his head and continued his efforts to sound at ease. 'Like I told you earlier, I think you're goin' to find a story here that'll make your trip worthwhile.'

'You have a fine reputation, Sheriff. When the Herald received your telegram they dispatched me to Tin Cup immediately.'

The compliment made Harry Clausen feel even more tense. He and the reporter began to walk to the Gold Coin Saloon for a prearranged meeting.

Inside the Gold Coin, the crowd was sparse, as it usually was at mid-morning. A few of the tables still had chairs on top of them as the swamper was finishing off his work.

Clausen viewed the scene with sadness. The swamper was Pop Cummings. In a few hours, Pop would start drinking. By early evening he'd be at his usual table, head down.

Sheriff Clausen's thoughts returned to the present. Three men sat at the only occupied table: Rance Dehner, Thad Brookshire and Foster Lewis. Lewis looked startled by the newcomers. He leaned back in his chair as if preparing for an attack.

Foster's discomfort helped Harry Clausen to feel a bit better: so far, so good. 'Gentlemen, I would like you to meet Mr Jim Harland, a reporter for the *Dallas Herald*.'

There were friendly handshakes from Dehner and Brookshire. Lewis seemed to shake Harland's hand with reluctance.

'Mr Lewis and I have already met,' Harland said. 'We both

started at the *Dallas Herald* at about the same time. Mr Lewis has since . . . ah . . . left the *Herald.* I believe you now work for a magazine, is that correct, Mr Lewis?'

Foster ignored the question and glared at Harry Clausen. 'Sheriff, you promised I would be the only writer at this meeting—'

'I promised no such thing, Mr Lewis—'

The sheriff's reply was interrupted as the batwings opened. Peter Kyle entered his own saloon accompanied by Reverend Levi Davis. The pastor was moving slowly and looked pale. Kyle remained close by Davis's side until he was seated at the table.

'How are you feeling, Reverend?' Rance asked.

'Better . . . better.'

'The Reverend is not being obedient,' Kyle joked as he sat down beside his friend. 'The doctor told him to stay in bed for at least another week.'

'I can't,' Davis responded. 'There's too much work to do. Much to the disappointment of Tin Cup's children, school will be back in session tomorrow.'

The pastor smiled at his own joke, then continued. 'I can't ride a horse yet, but one of my deacons will give me a ride on his buckboard out to the Rocking S. Abner Shaw is living a nightmare. He needs all the help the church and town can provide.'

The pastor's statement set a grim tone. Clausen and the reporter sat down at the table. The sheriff spoke in a low, serious tone. 'Tin Cup has been through a terrible ordeal. Three of our citizens were murdered. Reverend Davis was shot. It is important that the truth of this whole matter get out. The real truth. All this talk about a ghost and such needs to be stopped.'

The sheriff paused, fidgeted with his hands and then

continued. 'I think the answer is to have a meeting like the one we had planned to have in the church. Only this time we're not gonna fuss over what happened twenty years ago. No more of this ghost nonsense. We're gonna get out the facts about what's really been goin' on.'

Clausen paused again. He wasn't sure this part of the plan was going to work. 'I think you men will be able to explain what really went on in Tin Cup recently. Thad, why don't you start off by telling us how you became a deputy sheriff?'

Clausen was relieved when his deputy immediately began to speak. 'I had been fired from a job as a ranch hand. I was heading for Donahue's General Store to buy some supplies before I left town. I heard threatening voices—'

'Stop!' Foster Lewis shouted. 'Are you going to talk about that night I already wrote about in *Real Gunfighters*?'

'Yes, Mr Lewis, I am. And I'm going to be truthful.'

'You can't do that!' Lewis slammed a fist on the table. 'If the *Dallas Herald* prints a story that contradicts mine, I'll be a laughing stock. I'll get fired!'

'Maybe you should have thought about that, Mr Lewis, before writing all those fool lies.' Anger flared in Thad's eyes. Harry Clausen felt good. Thad Brookshire was starting to show some emotion.

So was Foster Lewis. The writer huffed loudly, stood up and stormed out of the Gold Coin. As soon as he had departed, most of the other men at the table began to guffaw.

Rance Dehner didn't laugh. He looked toward Clausen. 'Can you hold this meeting without me?'

The sheriff was still enjoying his amusement over Lewis's humiliation. 'Guess so. You gotta leave, Rance?'

'Yes.' Dehner got up and hastily exited the saloon.

Rance stood outside the Gold Coin and looked around. A man who has been humiliated is capable of creating a lot of misery and mayhem. Foster Lewis had just been humiliated, his dream of getting a huge story destroyed. And there had been something in the writer's face that spooked Rance. Lewis was a man who desperately needed success, and that success had just come under serious threat.

The detective spotted Lewis coming out of a gunshop, far down the boardwalk from where Dehner was standing. The writer carried something, but Rance couldn't see it clearly.

Dehner followed far behind Lewis. The writer walked in a fast manner to Abbot's Livery. Rance got close enough to the Livery's open front doors to hear Lewis paying for a horse and saddle he had just rented.

The detective scurried around the corner of the stable which proved an unnecessary precaution. Lewis didn't look around at all as he rode off. He was a man on a mission.

Dehner hurried into the livery. Stanley Abbot's son, a 15-year-old version of his father, was standing at an old battered desk, putting away the money he had just received. 'Howdy Mr Dehner! Need your horse?'

'Yes, and I need him in a hurry.'

CHAPTER TWENTY-FOUR

Foster Lewis guided his buckskin towards a dilapidated shack beside a corral containing two bony horses. A flurry of emotions possessed the writer. He had heard those men laughing at him. People were always laughing at him. Well, this time it would be different – a lot different.

Lewis's thoughts were interrupted by the sound of three gunshots. He dismounted and tied the buckskin to the corral. The smell of moonshine was in the air, but Lewis couldn't see where the still was located and didn't really care. His attention was focused on the man trying to shoot rocks off a log.

Walking in a slow, cautious manner, Lewis approached the shooter. 'Hello, Boone.'

Boone turned and faced the newcomer with suspicion. Boone looked upon everyone with suspicion. He lived a life of bare survival in which there were no friends.

'I know ya,' he said. Lewis couldn't tell if it was a question or a statement.

'Sure,' Lewis responded with a forced cheerfulness. 'We first met in the Hotel Lobby. You sold me a jug. Then, a few days ago, I brought you that gun. Remember? You said the Colt .45 sure beat that old thing you had.'

Boone pointed the gun at Lewis but not in a threatening manner. 'You said you'd put me in a mager—'

'Magazine. Yes.'

Boone holstered his gun. 'Ah cain't read yet, but ah heard 'bout the magerzine with the Lightning Kid. I'm faster'n him.'

'I know. And we're going to prove it tonight!'

Boone twitched and began to scratch his head vigorously. Lewis reckoned Boone Estey had lice. The writer figured his timing was opportune. Boone could still follow directions. In another year or so, the tanglefoot would have totally addled the moonshiner's brain.

'You have family here?'

'My pa and me.'

'I may need his help tonight.'

'How come?'

Foster ignored the question. 'Can't believe the Lightning Kid has been made a deputy. What was that fool sheriff thinking?'

'Don't know nothin' about it.'

'I'll bet in no time the Lightning Kid will be out here trying to close you and your pa down.'

'The sheriff leaves us alone, long as we don't cause no trouble.'

'The Lightning Kid is different from the sheriff.'

'How's that?'

'He's the son of a rich man! You know how rich people act, they're always causing trouble for the poor.'

Anger suddenly oozed from Boone's eyes. 'You're right! Them rich men who own the saloons, they make it hard for us to sell our jugs.'

Foster grabbed at the opening. 'And the men who own the saloons control the Lightning Kid. He does whatever they want.'

'I ain't afraid of the Lightning kid.'

'Of course not. You're faster than him and, like I said,

you're going to prove it tonight.'

'How?'

As Foster explained his plan, he felt pleased that Boone was obviously going along with it, but he didn't feel all that good about Boone's chances against Thad Brookshire. The plan would need some modification to ensure that the Lightning Kid was killed by the gun of a poor man.

Foster Lewis stood on the boardwalk across from the Gold Coin. He was trying to appear inconspicuous and failing. The task was impossible with Boone Estey beside him.

'My pa did right, earned his pay,' Boone spoke as if someone had accused his father of stealing money. 'Got the sheriff and that Dehna guy outta town with a loco story 'bout—'

'Keep your voice down!' Foster looked around, relieved to see that no one was close by. 'The deputy will be starting the evening round soon. It'll be the usual routine, he'll enter the Gold Coin, go to the bar and ask the bartender if everything is OK.'

'That's when I kill him,' Boone's voice was now a whisper, a loud whisper, but a whisper.

Lewis wished he had found someone else to be his hero. Too late now. 'You'll walk into the saloon, say, "Deputy, you aren't pushing around the poor people in this town any longer" and walk to the end of the bar. Be sure you are on the end near the wall with the window in it.'

'I can outdraw the Lightnin' Kid.' Boone's voice was less certain than it had been only a few hours ago.

'Sure you can! But don't worry, I'll be backing you up. Now, stay here, stay quiet and wait for the deputy to walk into the Gold Coin.' Lewis patted the moonshiner on the back before making his way across the road and through the bat wing doors.

Lewis gave the saloon a long glance. The Gold Coin looked typical for early in the evening. There were several people scattered about and that old man, the one they called Pop-something was passed out at his usual table.

The big crowd was still an hour or so away, so the writer had his pick of which lady to use for his scheme. He purposely chose the least attractive saloon girl available. She was grossly overweight with a red mustache created by sloppily applied lipstick. Her blond hair was obviously a wig and obviously not new.

'Let's you and me go upstairs first and then I'll buy you a drink.'

The woman, used to being the last selected, looked surprised, but accompanied Foster up a wide stairway on the far side of the bar. The stairs led to the second floor rooms where business was conducted.

'Keep walking,' Lewis instructed as blonde wig stopped at the first room they came to. The couple walked around the horseshoe shaped second floor balcony and past several rooms until they arrived at a very short corridor at the end of the horseshoe. The corridor contained one room. Foster handed the woman a couple of bills. 'Get inside the room. Don't come out till I tell you.'

The woman shrugged her shoulders and did what she was told. Foster Lewis settled into a dark corner of the corridor where he had an excellent view of the saloon floor below.

No one could spot him unless they looked carefully and no one would be looking. He had purposely chosen blond wig because one of the more attractive girls might have gotten some leering glances as she traversed the second floor.

Now he only had to wait. Foster caressed the .45 which was tucked into his belt. He had purchased the gun earlier in the day: a gun identical to the one he had given to Boone Estey.

Foster smiled, the name wasn't Boone Estey anymore. It was Hardscrabble. Lewis was proud of the new handle he had created for his new hero. Hardscrabble would be a name that stood for a man who used his speed with a gun to help the poor.

The writer allowed himself a quiet chuckle. Hardscrabble's fight for the poor was going to make a certain writer rich. He would marry Mitzi and live the kind of life they both wanted and deserved.

More customers were moseying into the Gold Coin. Good. The more people, the more confusion. After the shooting was over, he would go downstairs and start planting notions in people's minds as to what had happened. It had always worked before.

Foster pulled the .45 from his belt. This gunfight was too important. He couldn't leave anything to chance. He would gun down the Lightning Kid himself. The kid just might kill Hardscrabble. In a way, that might be for the best. Poor boy kills rich tyrant and takes a fatal bullet himself. Not bad at all. . . .

Thad Brookshire shouldered his way through the bat wings. The deputy exchanged a few hellos with some of the customers as he made his way towards the bar.

'The new job treating you OK, Max?'

'Sure,' the bartender replied. 'Everything is—'

Boone Estey stomped into the saloon. 'Lightnin' Kid, you stop jawin' 'bout me bein' poor, 'cause I ain't.'

Foster Lewis cringed. His hope that Boone would end up dead ratcheted up a notch.

Thad gave the newcomer a relaxed smile. 'Take it easy, friend. Let me buy you a drink.'

Boone looked confused. For a horrible moment, Lewis feared the moonshiner might accept the free drink.

'No! I want nothin' from ya.' Lewis smiled with relief as he watched Boone position himself at the end of the bar facing the deputy. Once the gunfight began, Thad Brookshire would be in perfect range for Foster Lewis's shot from the balcony.

Once again, the crowd in the Gold Coin lined themselves safely away from any potential bullet, but close enough to see the show. Foster Lewis took a few cautious steps towards the railing. As soon as Thad Brookshire went for his gun, Lewis would kill him.

'I ain't afraid of ya!' Boone shouted. Perspiration cut a trail from his forehead through his cheeks.

'I didn't say you were.' Thad kept his voice low and calm.

'I'm countin' ta three, then ya better draw. One—'

Rance Dehner broke loose from the crowd huddled against the wall and approached Boone from behind. 'Can you sell me a jug of tanglefoot?'

Boone looked startled. Dehner grabbed the moonshiner by his shoulder, twirled him around and landed a hard right to the side of his head. Boone Estey hit the floor, his shiny new Colt still in its holster.

Pop Cummings suddenly stood up from his table, only it wasn't Pop, it was Harry Clausen with a six shooter in hand which he pointed at Lewis. 'Hands up, right now!'

Foster Lewis felt dizzy and disoriented. He had to act fast. He'd bring down the sheriff first and then kill Brookshire. Then he'd make up a story. . . .

Lewis aimed his gun at Clausen but felt a sharp burn in his chest before he could pull the trigger. The writer staggered backwards, trying desperately to keep his balance. He fired his .45 but the bullet went into the floor only a few feet from him.

The harsh noise resounded in his ears and Foster Lewis realized he was dying. 'Mitzi,' he whispered the name twice, realizing he would never see her again. Then a terrifying realization coursed through him.

Mitzi didn't care. She didn't care that he was dying. Mitzi wouldn't miss him at all when he didn't show at the Crystal Palace. The woman he loved wouldn't give him a thought.

Foster Lewis staggered forward and fell over the railing. His body did a graceful turn in the air before he hit the floor on his back. As Dehner crouched over the writer, he was struck by the thought that Lewis's fall looked like something from one of his articles.

But Foster Lewis would not be writing any more articles. 'This man is dead,' Rance said to the sheriff.

The three lawmen left the saloon along with Boone Estey. Harry Clausen spoke to the moonshiner in a low, angry voice. 'Boone, you're gonna take off that gun of yours right now and give it to me. I better never see you wearin' a gun in town again.'

'Gun is mine,' Boone spoke as he stroked his head. He had a headache from the blow he had taken from Dehner, but Boone Estey was used to headaches.

The sheriff's eyebrows shot up and the anger in his voice intensified. 'OK, Boone, I'll see you get everythin' that's comin' to you. You just tried to call out a deputy sheriff. I can charge you with a whole bunch of stuff. Same with your daddy for lyin' to the law. Now, I'm gonna ask Rance Dehner here to count to ten. If your Colt .45 isn't in my hands when he finishes, I'm takin' you to jail.'

Boone parted with the gun just as Dehner reached seven.

The moonshiner's shoulders twitched. 'Can I still sell

my jugs in town?'

If Clausen's anger subsided, he didn't show it. 'Boone, that all depends on what kind of mood I'm in and right now I'm feeling pretty ornery. Where's your horse?'

'Tied up at the side of the livery. Don't have to pay there.'

'Get on it and get outta town. Don't come back for a few weeks, then maybe I'll be feelin' a mite more charitable.'

Boone weaved away. The three lawmen watched him for a few moments and then, confident Estey was leaving town, they headed for the sheriff's office.

'Good thing you followed Lewis and overheard his crazy plans, Rance.' Clausen was in the middle of the threesome. 'Gave us a chance to come up with a plan of our own. Havin' me pose as Pop Cummin's was a good idea. I could watch that fool writer from the moment he stepped into the Gold Coin.'

'All this is pretty much over now,' Thad's voice sounded nervous. His words collided with each other and were hard to understand.

'Come again?' The sheriff asked.

Thad still appeared nervous, but his speech became clear. 'This whole Jimmy Ellis matter is finished. Once that article appears in the *Dallas Herald* people will know there never was a ghost. Amanda . . . all the people responsible for the killings are dead or in jail. There's nothing more to do.'

Clausen smiled broadly, but he didn't look happy. 'Guess you're right about that.'

'Earlier today I was talking with Rance.' Thad's eyes had been skirting about. He turned and faced the sheriff directly. 'Now that everything is settled, I need to get back to Dallas to see my father and sister. Rance and I thought we'd leave in the morning.'

'Sure,' Clausen said as they arrived at the sheriff's office.

Thad spoke as the sheriff opened the office door. 'Guess I'll go over to the livery and make sure Boone Estey leaves town.' The deputy hurried off.

Sheriff Clausen watched his young deputy walk briskly away. His voice became heavy with artificial casualness. 'Do you suppose he's goin' to Dallas for good or just for a visit?'

'I don't know,' Dehner replied. 'And right now, I don't think Thad knows.'

CHAPTER TWENTY-FIVE

Morning was crowding out the night, but an ample moon still clung to the sky. Both Dehner and Thaddeus Brookshire were checking the saddlebags on their horses. Their steeds were tied to the hitching rail outside the sheriff's office.

Rance looked at the young man who seemed nervous as he patted his chestnut. 'Are you looking forward to seeing your father, Thad?'

'Yes. Say, do you suppose the doctors could be wrong? I mean. . . .'

'William Brookshire is a tough man, Thad. He may fool those doctors.'

'Yes, Dad is tough, sort of like Harry Clausen.' Thad's eyes became distant. 'Harry and my father are both strong men, strong in very different ways.'

'We should go inside and say our good-byes to the sheriff.'

As the two men entered the office, Harry Clausen looked up from his desk. The gesture appeared a bit artificial and Rance figured the sheriff hadn't really been engrossed in paper work.

'Morning, gents!' Harry's voice was loud and friendly.

'Good morning, Sheriff,' Thad shot back.

'Say, I've been thinkin',' Harry Clausen leaned back in his chair. 'You two have sure been a big help to me. So, let me pay you back some. I'll buy you both breakfast before you head out.'

Thad's eyes shot to the floor, but only for a second. He looked up at the man behind the desk. 'Thanks Sheriff, but we got a lot of riding to do and we need to get started.'

'Sure!' Clausen stood up, waving a hand as if dismissing the offer. 'Just because I'm always thinking about my stomach, doesn't mean you gents are.'

Awkward laughter filled the room.

Thad's face began to contort. 'I'm sorry to be leaving you like this, Sheriff, without a deputy and all.'

'You're doin' the right thing, boy.' Clausen's voice was firm. 'You need to visit your pa.'

'It's more than a visit.' Thad took the badge off his shirt and placed it reverently on the desk. 'I'm not coming back.'

Harry Clausen stared downward at the small piece of tin. His face was devoid of all emotion. Dehner knew that was exactly how the lawman wanted it.

Clausen suddenly laughed and gave his companions a wide smile. 'I wondered how long it would take you to smarten up, Thad! Why, there's no future bein' a small town lawdog. You belong back in Dallas where there's all sorts of opportunities for you.'

Thad smiled slightly, but his voice remained serious. 'You've taught me a lot, Sheriff.'

Clausen shrugged his shoulders. 'An old lawdog like me don't know all that much to teach.'

'You taught me the special qualities a man needs to wear a badge,' Thad said. 'I don't have those qualities and neither does my dad. My dad saw a lot of killing during the war and I've seen more than enough killing in this town. I ended the life of a man who wanted to kill me so he'd get his name in a magazine! No. I'm like my father. I want to be a man who builds things. I can't be the man who protects the builders.'

Thad pressed his lips together, as if not sure he should say any more. Then he spoke with a new force in his voice. 'And another thing, Sheriff, you didn't rawhide me at all for being such a fool over Amanda. I let myself be conned by a pretty face. I may be eighteen, but I still have some growing up to do.'

The smile on Clausen's face became smaller but more genuine. 'I think you've done a lot of growin' up already.'

'I'll write you a letter and let you know what's going on,' Thad said.

'Thanks, I'll look forward to that.' Clausen looked about in a jerky manner, then spoke to Rance with overblown, comical anger. 'Dehner, I don't care if you do work cheap, next time I see you in Tin Cup, I'm goin' to run you out. You're nothin' but trouble.'

The three men laughed and continued to make jokes as they left the office. Rance and Thad quickly mounted their horses and began to ride out of town. As they did so, they turned and waved to Harry Clausen who was standing in the middle of the road.

At the edge of town, Dehner turned back and saw the sheriff who once again began waving at them vigorously.

Rance waved again and sensed that Harry Clausen was hoping Thad would turn and wave to him. Rance glanced at the young man riding beside him. Thaddeus Brookshire was looking straight forward, his mind obviously on thoughts of Dallas and his family. It seemed wrong to intrude.

Dehner turned around one last time. Maybe it was just the clouds passing over a fading moon, but Harry Clausen's body seemed to slump a bit as he returned to his office.